The Illusion Of Us

Krista Lastella

ABOUT THE AUTHOR

Krista Lastella, also known as KLastella, is an aspiring author who lives in the US with her loving and supportive husband, their happy and very energetic little girl, and their adorable golden retriever named Mochi (sticky rice).

Krista is passionate about crafting stories that either tug at her readers' hearts or drive them mad. With a particular knack for writing angst-filled tales, she thrives on exploring deep, emotional narratives. Though she acknowledges that she still has much to learn, her wide imagination ensures she never runs out of stories to tell.

Her goal is to connect with readers through her unique voice and compelling plots, leaving them eagerly anticipating her next creation.

You can follow the author on her social media accounts:

Instagram: @klastella06
Facebook Page: klastella06

TABLE OF CONTENTS

CHAPTER ONE

"I'm getting married!" Ava exclaimed, her voice bubbling with excitement as she displayed her 5-carat diamond engagement ring to her friends at the King Cole Bar. Ethan was nearby, sharing in the joyous moment.

Her girlfriends gasped in awe at the sight of the ring. "OMG, Ava! You two finally did it! Congratulations!" Amy, her best friend since their first year of college, said with a burst of excitement, pulling Ava into a tight hug. "Oh, I'm so happy for you!"

"Thank you, Amy!" Ava returned the warmth of her friend's embrace, her smile wide and genuine. In the background, she could hear their other friends offering their congratulations to Ethan.

"So, how did Ethan propose?" Jasmine, another college friend, asked curiously, sipping her apple martini.

Ava glanced over at her boyfriend, now fiancé, with a giggle. "Babe, do you want to tell them, or should I?" she asked, looping her arms around him. He mirrored her affectionate gesture, their comfort with public displays of affection evident.

"You should, babe. You're great at storytelling," Ethan replied, planting a sweet kiss on her forehead. Their friends watched, squealing with delight at the couple's evident happiness.

Ava went on to tell their friends how Ethan had proposed to her the previous night in front of her parents. It was a candid moment, yet deeply romantic for her, fulfilling her long-held wish to have her parents present during the proposal. Ethan had made that dream come true.

Their romance had begun at the age of 20, when both attended the same university. Initially, Ava had a significant crush on Ethan but thought he was more interested in her friend, Violet, due to the attention he seemed to give her. Consequently, she had distanced herself from him. To Ava's surprise, Ethan had chosen to pursue her instead of Violet, turning their friendship into a blossoming romance. They quickly became one of the most admired couples on campus and had remained deeply in love ever since.

Years after graduating from college, many around them had expected an engagement, yet Ethan hadn't proposed. There were times when Ava wondered if he really wanted to marry her, but she later discovered that Ethan had been waiting to finish his internship before proposing. Ethan had recently started his residency at Greenwood Medical Center.

Ethan's residency at Greenwood Medical Center wasn't just a professional milestone; it was a convergence of his personal life with a prestigious medical legacy. The hospital, established by Ava's grandfather Jameson Greenwood Sr., was a pillar in the medical community, renowned for its excellence and the lineage of surgeons it had produced.

THE ILLUSION OF US

Ava's family had long been intertwined with the history of Greenwood Medical Center. Her father, James Greenwood, held the esteemed position of chairman, having previously served as the chief of surgery. Her older brother, Nate, continued the family tradition as the chief of the Cardiology Department, and her mother was renowned for her tenure as the chief of general surgery.

Despite the deep medical roots of her family, her passion led her to the world of patisserie, a craft she pursued with the same dedication and excellence her family showed in medicine. Ava had just celebrated the opening of her second La Belle Époque Patisserie branch.

When Ava and Ethan's relationship blossomed, it was more than just a personal connection; it was the joining of two families with deep ties to Greenwood Medical Center. Ava's father, James, was overjoyed upon learning that she was dating Ethan, seeing the union as a harmonious blending of past and present. Ethan, the son of Harry Williams, the current chief of surgery and an old friend of James, was already well-regarded in the Greenwood family.

"Finally, after six years, you two are actually getting married," Tony remarked as they sipped their drinks. Tony, Ethan's best friend, appeared genuinely happy for them.

They all raised their glasses, toasting to the engaged couple's future. "You both deserve each other, and I'm thrilled to see that after so many years, your relationship is stronger than ever," Amy added with enthusiasm. Even though she was slightly tipsy, her sincerity was evident, and her boyfriend Carlson was there supporting her.

"Thank you, everyone. Your support means so much to us," Ethan responded, visibly moved by the genuine happiness and well-wishes of their friends for their engagement.

As the evening continued, the King Cole Bar was alive with the laughter and chatter of the group. The air was filled with a sense of celebration, each toast and cheer bringing Ava and Ethan closer to the reality of their impending nuptials. The glow of the engagement ring on Ava's finger seemed to sparkle even brighter with each story and memory shared among friends.

Music played softly in the background, adding to the ambiance. The group reminisced about their college days, the adventures they had shared, and the journey that Ava and Ethan had embarked on together. Each anecdote brought smiles and sometimes even tears of joy.

As the night wore on, the group's energy gradually shifted from high-spirited to a more reflective mood. Ava found herself leaning into Ethan, feeling an overwhelming sense of gratitude and love. In that moment, surrounded by their closest friends, the challenges of the past and the dreams for the future all seemed to intertwine.

Eventually, the night began to wind down. Tony, ever the joker, made a few lighthearted jokes about wedding planning, eliciting laughter and eye rolls. Amy, leaning on Carlson for support, expressed her excitement about being involved in the wedding preparations.

Ethan, holding Ava's hand under the table, gave it a gentle squeeze. Their eyes met, sharing a silent conversation filled with love and anticipation for the life they were about to build together. As they left the bar, the cool night air felt refreshing, the city lights twinkling like distant stars, mirroring the joy and hope in their hearts.

The evening at King Cole Bar was more than just a celebration of an engagement; it was a reaffirmation of love, friendship, and the journeys yet to come. Ava and Ethan walked away feeling cherished and supported, ready to step into the next chapter of their lives.

After bidding their friends farewell at the bar, Ethan and Ava made their way to Central Park for a tranquil walk. The park was a vision, adorned with twinkling Christmas lights that cast a magical glow. They strolled hand in hand, their presence complementing the serene beauty around them.

Ethan, with his striking features and warm, inviting eyes, looked at Ava thoughtfully. The soft lights of the park accentuated his handsome countenance, the gentle expression on his face reflecting his deep affection for her. "So, what are your dreams for our wedding?" he asked, his voice as soothing as the night around them.

Ava, radiant in the ethereal light, her eyes sparkling with excitement, turned to him. Her beauty was effortless, a natural glow that seemed to light up the space around her. "I've always imagined an outdoor wedding," she responded, her voice carrying the melody of her joy. "A garden setting, surrounded by flowers. What do you think?"

Ethan's smile deepened, his handsome features glowing in the soft light. "That sounds like a dream. I just want it to be a day that makes you happy," he said, his gaze lingering on Ava's face, admiring the way the light danced across her delicate features.

Ava's eyes shone with a mix of love and thoughtfulness. "I've been thinking... I don't want a grand wedding," she began. "Something intimate, with only our family and closest friends. I want each moment to feel personal and special."

Ethan nodded in understanding. "I agree. It's not about the size of the wedding, but the memories we create. With a smaller ceremony, we can really focus on us and the people who have supported our journey.

"There's a certain charm in simplicity, isn't there?" Ava mused. "A beautiful garden, our loved ones around us, and just the essence of our love. That's all we really need."

"Exactly," Ethan replied, his voice warm. "And we'll make sure every detail reflects us, our story. What about the music? Any thoughts on that?"

Ava smiled, her mind drifting to melodies. "I'd love a string quartet, something romantic and timeless. Maybe they could play our song as I walk down the aisle?"

"I love that idea," Ethan said, his eyes twinkling with excitement. "And for our first dance, let's choose a song that's been significant throughout our relationship."

As they continued their stroll, their conversation flowed effortlessly, delving into various aspects of their upcoming wedding. They talked about their favorite flowers for the bouquet, the ideal menu for the reception, and even joked about their dance moves. The night air was filled with their laughter and dreams, the festive lights of Central Park witnessing the deepening bond between them. In those moments, the world seemed to stand still, allowing Ava and Ethan to savor the joy of planning their future together.

CHAPTER TWO

Ethan and Ava were cuddled together in their bed, basking in the warmth as they watched the snowflakes gently fall outside. Ava had always been enchanted by snow; every time it snowed, she would draw back the curtains of their expansive glass window, allowing her to watch the snowfall until she drifted into sleep.

"This is perfect..." Ava whispered, snuggling closer into Ethan's broad shoulder. His natural scent was like a signature perfume to her, comforting and familiar. Wrapped in his arms, she felt an overwhelming sense of security and love.

Ethan, with Ava's hand resting on his chest, smiled tenderly. "You've always loved being held like this, babe. It seems to be the magic trick to get you to sleep," he said with a soft chuckle. His laughter was like music to her ears, adding to the tranquility of the moment.

"Are you complaining, Mister Ethan Williams?" Ava teased playfully, looking up at him. "Remember, you're the one who got me used to this." She then playfully tickled his side, causing him to burst into laughter.

Their playful banter quickly turned into a tickle fight, both of them leaping out of bed and engaging in a joyous, childlike game. Since moving into their Manhattan apartment two years ago, Ethan and Ava's life together had been filled with such moments of spontaneous joy and happiness. Their home was a haven of love and laughter, a perfect world they had created together, away from the rest of the world.

As they paused, panting and laughing from their playful escapade, they shared a look that conveyed unspoken words. In that instant, Ethan closed the distance between them, capturing her lips with a kiss that spoke of deep longing. Ava responded with equal fervor, the intensity of their kiss reigniting a familiar, passionate flame.

Before they knew it, they found themselves back on the bed, lost in the heat of the moment. The room was filled with the sounds of their shared desire, an unbridled expression of their love and connection. The world outside faded away as they became wholly absorbed in each other, their bond as strong and fiery as ever.

Exhausted yet content, they lay there catching their breath after a night filled with passion. Neither had the energy to get dressed; instead, they simply pulled the blanket over themselves, covering their bare skin. Ava snuggled back against Ethan, who warmly wrapped his arms around her once more.

"I love you, Ethan," she whispered, her eyelids growing heavy with the pull of sleep.

He responded with a gentle kiss on her forehead. "I love you too, babe." In the comfort of each other's embrace, they both drifted off to sleep, a perfect end to their night together.

The morning sun streamed through the curtains of Ava and Ethan's bedroom, casting a warm glow over the room. Ava slowly opened her eyes, the clock on the bedside table showing that they had overslept. "Babe, wake up! We overslept!" she exclaimed, gently shaking him awake.

Ethan jolted upright, a look of surprise on his handsome face. "What? Oh no, I have an early shift at the hospital!" he blurted out, scrambling out of bed in a hurry.

The bedroom was suddenly a flurry of activity, with both of them rushing to get ready. Ava dashed to the kitchen to quickly make some breakfast. "Toast it is!" she declared, popping slices of bread into the toaster while Ethan hurriedly got dressed in the other room.

Ethan emerged from the bedroom, trying to tie his tie while simultaneously searching for his hospital badge. "Have you seen my badge?" he asked in a slightly panicked tone.

"Check the living room, I think you left it there last night!" Ava called out from the kitchen, flipping the toasts onto plates.

Ethan, finding his badge on the coffee table, let out a relieved sigh. "Found it!" he announced, rushing back to the kitchen.

Ava handed him a plate of toast, trying to suppress a laugh at his disheveled hair. "You might want to give your hair a quick comb," she teased.

He glanced at his reflection in the toaster. "I look like a mad scientist," he joked, quickly trying to tame his hair with his fingers.

They shared a quick, affectionate kiss, laughter still in their eyes. "Have a great day, Dr. Williams," Ava said with a playful salute.

"You too, babe," Ethan replied, grabbing his toast and rushing out the door.

Ava watched him go, a smile on her face. Despite the rush, mornings like these were filled with a simple, joyful chaos that she cherished. With a contented sigh, she grabbed her own breakfast and headed out, ready to tackle the day at her patisserie. The hurried start only added to the charm of their busy, happy life together.

As Ethan dove into the demands of his residency, Ava found herself immersed in the whirlwind of wedding planning. With Ethan entrusting her with the decision-making, she embraced the role with enthusiasm and creativity.

The journey of finding the perfect wedding venue turned into a bonding experience for Ava, her mother, and Ethan's mom. They spent several weekends visiting potential sites, each with its own unique charm and appeal.

"I want it to feel like we're stepping into a midsummer night's dream, even though it's winter," Ava said with a determined smile as they entered the grand conservatory. The indoor space was a masterful emulation of a lush garden, with rich greenery and vibrant flowers in full bloom, all under the shelter of a translucent glass dome that let in soft, natural light.

Her mother nodded in approval, "An indoor garden setting is perfect for a winter wedding. It's cozy and warm but still has the charm of an outdoor celebration."

As they toured the conservatory, Ethan's mother was drawn to a delicate gazebo adorned with ivy and twinkling lights. "This could be a magical spot for the ceremony," she remarked, the warmth in the conservatory making it easy to forget the chill of winter outside.

They discussed everything from the ceremony layout to the reception arrangement, scrutinizing every detail. Venue coordinators presented them with various options, talking them through seating configurations, dance floor placements, and lighting that would create the perfect enchanted evening ambiance.

Upon discovering the venue that seemed to check all their criteria, a wave of elation swept through them. It was a graceful indoor sanctuary that brought the essence of summer gardens into a winter setting, with elegant ballrooms that opened up to vistas of frosted nature. The enthusiastic venue coordinator offered a detailed tour of the spaces.

Ava's mother, thinking ahead, suggested, "Why not use a combination of tall willow branches and low floral arrangements for the tables? It would make the room feel like an enchanted forest."

Ethan's mother, perusing a portfolio of floral decorations, pointed out an arrangement. "Imagine these white roses and hellebores complemented with sprigs of holly and draped ivy—it would be like a winter garden brought to life."

Ava's eyes gleamed with the image in her mind. "And if we add strings of soft white lights among the greenery, it would look like a starlit garden," she added excitedly.

The coordinator jotted down every detail with precision. "We'll capture the warmth and beauty of a garden in full bloom, ensuring your winter wedding is nothing short of a fairy tale," she assured them, as they planned to bring the magic of the outdoors into their winter nuptials.

Feeling content with their choices, they concluded the day with a celebratory lunch, excitedly talking about the next steps in the planning process. The venue had been chosen, a canvas ready to be painted with the colors of Ava and Ethan's love story.

In their cozy living room, Ava and Ethan were surrounded by a sea of wedding catalogs and lists. As they sifted through names and designs, Ava couldn't help but notice the weariness in Ethan's eyes, a testament to his long hours at the hospital.

"You know, you don't have to help with the invitations right now," Ava said gently, concern lacing her voice. "You're always so exhausted after your shifts. Maybe you should rest."

Ethan looked at her, a soft smile playing on his lips. "Baby, I might be tired, but being here with you, helping plan our wedding, it's the best part of my day. Seeing you so excited and happy about our wedding preparations... it means everything to me."

Ava's heart swelled at his words. "Are you sure? I don't want to add more to your plate."

"I'm sure," he assured her, his hand reaching out to caress hers. "Besides, I can't let you have all the fun. I want to be part of this too, every step of the way."

Reassured by his words, Ava smiled, her eyes shining with love. They returned to their task, discussing the old university gang and Ethan's cousins from Ohio. As they finalized the guest list, Ethan suggested a classic design for the invitations, with a nod to their garden theme.

"That's perfect," Ava agreed, her mind already racing with ideas. "And since we're getting married on Valentine's Day, maybe we can subtly incorporate a love theme?"

"February 14th, our day of love," Ethan echoed fondly. "I can't think of a better date for us."

As the evening wore on, they decided to cover the cost of their wedding party's attire, a gesture of gratitude towards their closest friends and family. Ethan's unwavering support and willingness to share in every detail of the planning filled Ava with an immense sense of gratitude and love.

Their discussion was more than just about invitations and attire; it was a tender exchange of support and partnership. Each decision, each moment spent planning together, only deepened their bond, a beautiful testament to their journey towards a life shared as one.

The cake tasting at Ava's patisserie, La Belle Époque, was not just another wedding task, but a delightful adventure. As the owner, Ava took pride in showcasing her establishment's best offerings. The shop, with its cozy ambience and inviting aroma of freshly baked goods, was a testament to her passion and skill.

"Welcome to my favorite part of the shop," Ava said with a bright smile, leading Ethan to a beautifully set tasting area. A variety of cakes, each a work of art, awaited their verdict.

"Let's start with the classic vanilla," Ava suggested, her eyes sparkling with excitement. She expertly sliced a piece, offering it to Ethan. His reaction was immediate delight.

"This is heavenly," Ethan commented, savoring each bite. "But we have a lot more to taste, right?"

"Absolutely," Ava replied, her laughter echoing in the warm space. They moved on to a rich chocolate cake, a tangy lemon zest delight, a lusciously layered strawberry, and even a bold caramel sea salt.

With each sample, the decision became increasingly difficult. Ethan, with a teasing glimmer in his eyes, exclaimed, "They're all so incredible! How can we possibly choose just one?"

Ava, thoughtfully tapping a fork against her lip, said, "What if we create a cake that represents both of us? A blend of our favorite flavors?"

Inspired, they envisioned a multi-tiered cake that symbolized their union. The final design was a culinary masterpiece – a bottom layer of sumptuous chocolate, a middle tier of smooth vanilla, and a top tier of exquisite raspberry filling, each one an embodiment of their shared tastes and experiences.

As they tasted and laughed, Ava's staff looked on fondly, sharing in the couple's joy. The decision to have the wedding cake made by La Belle Époque added a personal touch to their special day.

As they prepared to leave, Ava's heart swelled with happiness. "This was perfect. Thank you for being here, for making every step of this journey so special," she said, her hand finding his.

Ethan squeezed her hand gently, "There's nowhere else I'd rather be."

Before they exited, Ava turned to him with a hopeful expression. "Did you manage to take a day off next week? We need to visit the bridal boutique for my gown and your tuxedo."

Ethan nodded, his smile reassuring. "I wouldn't miss it for the world. I can't wait to see you find the perfect dress."

Hand in hand, they left the patisserie, each step they took together filled with love and anticipation for the life they were about to embark upon. It was moments like these – sweet, simple, and filled with love – that they cherished the most.

CHAPTER THREE

In the chic and elegant bridal boutique, Ava stepped into the spacious dressing room to try on her dream wedding gown. Meanwhile, Ethan, already dressed in his tuxedo, waited with bated breath.

The moment the dressing room curtain swept open, Ethan's eyes widened in awe. He stood there, impeccably dressed in a sharp black tuxedo. The jacket, with its sleek black lapel, hugged his frame perfectly, complementing his strong, lean physique. The crisp white shirt, black bow tie, and polished shoes added to his debonair appearance, making him the very picture of sophistication.

But it was Ava who stole the moment. She emerged, looking ethereal in a breathtaking fit-and-flare gown. The dress was a masterpiece of romantic and sexy lace, hugging her curves before flaring out into a voluminous skirt that cascaded beautifully to the floor. The intricate lacework was exquisitely detailed, interwoven with delicate beadwork that shimmered under the boutique's soft lighting.

Her hair was styled in a graceful updo, strands artfully framing her face, lending an air of elegance and sophistication. In her hands, she held a bouquet of white peonies and roses, a perfect complement to her stunning ensemble.

Ethan was speechless, his heart swelling with emotion at the sight of her. "B...Babe, you look... magnificent," he finally managed to say, his voice thick with emotion. The look in his eyes was one of pure adoration and love.

Ava's cheeks flushed with happiness, her eyes reflecting the love she felt. She twirled gently, the gown moving with her in a graceful dance, a vision of bridal beauty.

Slowly, Ethan leaned in, and their lips met in a tender, loving kiss. It was a moment that perfectly captured the essence of their journey – a symbol of their love and commitment.

Around them, the boutique staff watched, their faces lit up with smiles. A few couldn't help but let out soft giggles, charmed by the couple's display of affection. It was moments like these that brought a touch of real-life romance to their day-to-day work.

As Ethan and Ava broke the kiss, they looked around, slightly embarrassed but mostly filled with joy. They laughed, their hearts light, embracing not just each other but the entire experience.

"Looks like we're giving everyone here a bit of a show," Ethan joked, his eyes sparkling with happiness.

Ava, still in his arms and radiant in her gown, replied playfully, "Well, we are practicing for the big day, after all."

"I can't believe how lucky I am," he whispered, gazing into her eyes. "You are the most beautiful bride."

Ava, her eyes glistening with unshed tears of joy, replied softly, "And you are the most handsome groom. I can't wait to walk down the aisle to you."

In the bridal boutique, surrounded by mirrors and soft lights, Ethan and Ava shared a moment of profound connection, a beautiful prelude to their upcoming vows. The love they shared was palpable, filling the room with warmth and promise of a beautiful future together.

The excitement was just as intense as Ethan and Ava approached the luxurious Ritz-Carlton Bal Harbour in Miami, a stark contrast to the Hamptons but no less beautiful. Their friends were already gathered there, waiting to ring in the New Year with style and sea views that stretched endlessly.

As they pulled up, Amy, along with the rest of the gang, rushed towards them, their faces beaming with joy. "Finally, you're here!" Amy exclaimed, enveloping Ava in a warm hug.

"What took you so long?" she asked, her eyes twinkling with curiosity.

Ava laughed and playfully glanced at Ethan. "Ask him," she said, her laughter mixing with the salty sea breeze.

Ethan, with a sheepish grin, confessed, "I forgot where I put my car key, so we spent half the day looking for it." He ran a hand through his hair, adding, "Turns out, I left it inside the car."

The group erupted into laughter at his admission. "Someone is getting old," Tony teased, nudging Ethan playfully.

Ethan responded with a laugh and a light punch to Tony's belly. "Just a bit preoccupied," he said, his eyes meeting Ava's with a hint of something more behind them.

Ava had sensed Ethan's preoccupation lately. Whenever she asked, he'd dismiss it as 'nothing,' but she could tell his job at the hospital was weighing on him. This retreat at the Ritz-Carlton Bal Harbour was their much-needed escape, a chance for Ethan to relax.

As Ava and Amy walked back to the hotel, catching up on lost time, Ava looked over her shoulder at Ethan, who was managing their luggage. When their eyes met, she silently mouthed 'I love you,' and his smile back at her, along with the silent return of her words, was all the confirmation she needed of their unwavering connection.

This getaway in Miami was more than a festive gathering; it was a moment for Ethan and Ava to unwind, revel in the anticipation of their upcoming nuptials, and enjoy the warmth of their closest friends.

While Ethan retreated to their suite to recuperate from his demanding shifts and the journey, Ava joined the others for a day by the private beach. The guys took charge of the grill, while the ladies indulged in the sun's embrace, engaging in easy chatter.

"You seem really happy," Jasmine observed, glancing in Ava's direction, who was basking in the warm sunlight with a contented smile.

Amy, sipping her lemonade, looked over at Ava and chuckled. "Ava's always been the happy type, Jaz. She's like the only person who seems like she doesn't have a care in the world."

"Especially since she started dating Ethan. That smile has never left her face," Sofia added. She then turned to Ava, a curious look in her eyes. "Have you and Ethan ever had a fight? You two seem so perfect together."

Ava removed her sunglasses and grinned at her friends. "Well, Ethan just makes me incredibly happy. I can't explain it, but being with him makes everything seem brighter and lighter."

Sofia playfully nudged Ava. "Seriously, have you two ever had a disagreement? Like, over what flavor of cake to choose for the wedding?"

Ava laughed. "Well, there was this one time we debated over chocolate or vanilla. But we ended up choosing both, so no real fight there."

Fred, joining in from his spot on a nearby towel, called out, "That's the thing with you two. Even your disagreements are adorable."

Stef, reclining on her sun lounger, chimed in, "Remember when Ava and Ethan teamed up for game night last summer? They were like a mind-reading duo. Unbeatable!"

Amy, sipping her drink, added, "Yeah, and have you noticed how Ava's always humming or singing around Ethan? It's like she's got this permanent joy vibe going on."

Ava blushed slightly but nodded. "Ethan just has this way of making everything feel easy and joyful."

Jasmine, flipping through a magazine, looked up and said, "It's rare, you know, to see a couple so in sync with each other. You guys give us all relationship goals."

Markie, who had been quietly listening, spoke up, "I'll never forget when Ethan planned that surprise birthday party for Ava. The effort he put in to make her day special was something else."

Carlson, walking over from the grill, added with a smirk, "Yeah, but remember, no relationship is perfect. Like Amy and me – we argue over what show to binge-watch next."

Amy rolled her eyes playfully. "That's because your choices are terrible, hon."

The group erupted into laughter as their conversation continued, each friend sharing anecdotes and jokes about their relationships. The underlying theme was always the same – how Ava and Ethan seemed to be the perfect couple, always happy and in tune with each other.

As the sun began to set, casting a golden glow over the beach, the friends gathered closer, their bond strengthened by the shared laughter and stories. It was clear that for Ava and Ethan, their love was not just an inspiration to their friends, but a cherished, integral part of their own lives.

Ethan approached the group, a look of relaxed contentment on his face, and settled onto the chaise next to Ava. The laughter and chatter briefly paused as they all greeted him.

"Hey everyone, what are you all talking about?" he asked, stretching his legs comfortably.

Tony, sitting across from them with a beer in hand, replied,

"We were just reminiscing about our college days, dude. Remembering how immature we were back then."

Ava turned to Ethan, her smile bright and affectionate. "Hi babe, did you have a good sleep?"

He nodded, his eyes reflecting a deep sense of relaxation. "Yeah, I haven't slept this well in ages," he said, his voice light. His hands found Ava's shoulders, gently massaging them in a loving gesture.

Seizing the moment, Ava stood up and tugged at Ethan's hands. "Come on, let's go for a swim. You'll feel even better," she urged him, her tone playful.

Ethan allowed himself to be led, laughing as Ava playfully splashed water towards him. Soon, they were both in the water, Ethan chasing after Ava as she swam ahead, their laughter mingling with the sounds of the waves.

Their friends watched the couple with smiles, enjoying the sight of their playful, carefree love. Amy leaned over to Jasmine, "Look at them, always so full of life and love."

Jasmine nodded, her eyes on the couple. "They really are perfect together, aren't they?"

As Ethan finally caught up to Ava in the shallow surf, he swept her into his arms, spinning her around as the sunset draped the beach in a warm, golden light. The waves gently lapped at their feet, and the sound of the water mingling with their laughter created a perfect symphony of joy.

Ava's legs kicked playfully as she clung to Ethan, her hair whipped around by the sea breeze, a carefree smile lighting up her face. Ethan, strong and secure, held her effortlessly, the soft silhouette of their embrace against the fiery backdrop of the setting sun was like a scene from a beautiful dream.

Their friends watched from a distance, their figures mere shadows against the radiant sky, sharing knowing looks and smiles. This was more than just a playful chase in the water; it was a reflection of Ethan and Ava's love – vibrant, full of life, and beautiful in its sincerity.

As they stood in the water, Ethan gently set Ava back on her feet, but they remained close, wrapped in each other's arms. The sun dipped lower, the sky now streaked with colors of amber and purple, the ocean sparkling with the reflection of the day's last light. In this tranquil world, with the soft sand beneath them and the vast sky above, Ethan and Ava shared a tender, loving kiss, sealing their perfect day by the sea.

CHAPTER FOUR

As the final hours of the year ticked away, Ethan, Ava, and their close circle of friends gathered around a crackling bonfire on the beach. The fire's glow battled against the darkness, casting a warm, flickering light over everyone's faces. Logs popped and hissed, throwing sparks into the night like tiny fireworks.

The couples settled into cozy cuddles, blankets draped over their shoulders, as they each held a glass of wine, their favorite vintages brought especially for this moment. The air was filled with anticipation and the tang of sea salt mingled with the smoky scent of the bonfire.

"Okay, everyone, it's almost time!" Tony announced, checking his watch with excitement.

Amy, snuggled against Carlson, began the countdown. "Ten, nine, eight..."

The group joined in, their voices growing louder and more excited with each number.

"...three, two, one—Happy New Year!" they shouted in

unison, the beach echoing their cheer.

Glasses clinked in a symphony of crystal against crystal, wine splashing slightly over the rims in their eagerness. "To love, laughter, and friendship that lasts a lifetime!" Ava toasted, her eyes shining brightly as she leaned into Ethan's embrace.

"And to Ava and Ethan, may your upcoming wedding be as perfect as the two of you are together!" Jasmine added, raising her glass higher.

Laughter, cheers, and the soft murmur of New Year's resolutions being shared filled the air. The couples exchanged kisses, the single friends hugged, and everyone basked in the warmth of the fire and each other's company.

Sofia, always the jester, joked, "Now, let's make sure none of us do anything that ends up as a New Year's viral video, alright?"

The group erupted into laughter, knowing full well that their fun might just be memorable enough to break the internet. But that was a worry for another day. For now, they were content to be together, welcoming the New Year with open hearts and joyous spirits.

The group, still reveling in the warmth of their New Year's gathering, was jolted out of their cheerfulness by a sudden notification. It was a message on their long-dormant group chat, and the sender's name brought a wave of stunned silence: Violet.

She had been absent from their lives for six years after moving to France, leaving no digital trace behind. Her sudden text was a shock to them all.

Violet's message read: "Hey everyone, I'm coming home soon. Can't wait to catch up!"

Ava's eyes widened with a mix of shock and delight. "Look, it's Vi! She's coming back!" she exclaimed, her voice a cocktail of disbelief and joy.

The others crowded around the phone, re-reading the message as if to confirm its reality. "Violet? After all this time?" Amy muttered, a smile slowly breaking on their face.

"Violet? Is she serious?" Jasmine asked, breaking her silence.

Ava, her eyes shining with unshed tears, clutched her phone close. "I can't believe it. Vi's coming back. She might even be here for my wedding!" She was already lost in thoughts of reunion, her words tumbling out in a giddy rush.

The group began to buzz with speculation and excitement, each person voicing their surprise and theories on why Violet had suddenly decided to return. They reminisced about old times, their laughter resuming, albeit with a new, curious undertone.

"I wonder what brought her back after all these years," Amy pondered aloud, their tone laced with curiosity.

"Do you remember the last party we had with her?" Sofia chimed in, a nostalgic smile spreading across their face. "That was epic. She always knew how to make things fun."

"Yeah, and her sudden move to France? That was so like Violet, always full of surprises," Carlson added, laughing.

Meanwhile, Ethan remained silent, his expression distant. As the others speculated and laughed, his mind seemed to be elsewhere, perhaps entangled in a web of memories and emotions tied to Violet's unexpected message.

As the laughter and stories continued, Ava's gaze drifted to Ethan, who had been unusually quiet. His usual easygoing demeanor was replaced by a pensive silence.

"Ethan, you've barely said a word," Ava pointed out, her tone soft but curious. "You and Violet were always so close. Aren't you happy she's coming back?"

The room quieted down, as everyone's attention turned to Ethan. He seemed to struggle for a moment, looking for the right words.

"Yeah, it's... good news," Ethan replied, his voice hesitant. The lack of his usual enthusiasm didn't go unnoticed. "Just didn't expect to hear from her again, that's all."

Tony, observing Ethan's reaction, sensed there was something more behind his quietness. He recalled the close bond Ethan and Violet had shared and wondered if Ethan's silence was a reflection of unresolved feelings or a past that was still too tender to touch.

As the group's laughter and chatter filled the room, Tony kept his thoughts to himself, realizing that Ethan's subdued reaction to Violet's news was a private matter, something that perhaps only Ethan could understand and come to terms with in his own time. The joyous mood continued, but beneath the surface, there were layers of emotions and histories yet to be unraveled.

In their room, the festive atmosphere of the evening seemed a distant memory. Ethan's unusual behavior lingered in Ava's mind as she lay beside him on the bed. His silence was uncharacteristic, and his physical distance felt like an invisible barrier between them.

"Are you sure you're okay, baby?" Ava asked gently, her voice laced with concern. She watched Ethan closely, trying to read the emotions hidden behind his closed eyes.

There was a brief silence before Ethan responded, his voice weary. "I'm just tired, babe. I just want to sleep right now." His words were abrupt, cutting through the quiet of the room.

Ava nodded, though a flicker of worry crossed her face. "Oh, alright," she replied, her tone soft and understanding. She reached out, intending to offer a comforting kiss, but Ethan turned away, presenting his back to her.

A chill of unease crept into Ava's heart as her gesture was quietly rebuffed. It was unlike Ethan to dismiss her affection so bluntly. For a moment, she lay there, a tangle of anxiety and confusion clouding her thoughts.

But Ava shook off the negative feelings, attributing Ethan's behavior to sheer exhaustion and perhaps the unexpected news of Violet's return. She whispered a quiet "Good night, babe," into the darkness, hoping that sleep would bring back the warmth and closeness that had momentarily slipped away in the wake of Ethan's unspoken turmoil.

In the days following their vacation in Miami, life for Ethan and Ava had returned to its usual rhythm. The wedding preparations were proceeding without a hitch, and the couple found themselves in a comfortable routine. Tonight, they had planned a dinner with their parents, a casual check-in to discuss the wedding preparations, now just over a month away.

At the dinner, the atmosphere was warm and convivial, with Ethan and Ava's families gathered around the table. The conversation naturally steered towards the upcoming wedding.

"So, how's the wedding planning going?" Ava's mother asked, her eyes twinkling with excitement.

Ava beamed, "It's going great, Mom. We've got the venue and the caterer all set. And the dress... wait till you see it!"

Ethan chimed in with a smile, "Yeah, it's all coming together nicely. We're really looking forward to it." Ethan added, "And we've got the band sorted. They're really good."

Ethan's father, a man of few words, nodded approvingly. "Sounds like you've got it all under control. It's going to be a great day."

Ava's mother continued, "And Ava, your dress? I can't wait to see you in it."

Ava laughed, "It's a surprise, Mom. But I promise, you'll love it."

Her father raised his glass. "To Ava and Ethan, may your future be as bright and joyful as this occasion."

Everyone raised their glasses in agreement, the clink of glass echoing warmly in the room.

Nate, Ava's big brother, leaned forward with a mischievous

THE ILLUSION OF US

grin. "Just make sure you don't get cold feet, Ethan. You're getting a real gem here."

Ethan laughed, "No chance of that, Nate. I'm the lucky one here."

Ava's mother's gaze softened as she looked at them. "You two really are perfect for each other. We couldn't be happier."

Ava reached out and squeezed Ethan's hand under the table, a silent gesture of love and unity.

Ethan, though he smiled and engaged in the conversation, had a faraway look in his eyes for just a moment, a hint of the internal conflict he had been grappling with since the news of Violet's return.

The evening continued with more laughter and shared stories, the families bonding over shared memories and the excitement of the upcoming wedding. But beneath the surface, Ethan's momentary distant gaze lingered in Ava's mind, a subtle reminder of the unresolved emotions that still hung in the air.

It had been several weeks since Ava and Ethan last shared a passionate night or quality time together. Ethan's residency at the hospital kept him busier than ever, leaving little time for them as a couple. So, after a family dinner, Ava planned a special evening to give her fiancé a much-needed break.

Luckily, Ethan had to pick up some important papers at the hospital after dinner, giving Ava the perfect opportunity to prepare a romantic surprise at their apartment. She hurriedly scattered rose petals from the front door to their bedroom, which she'd kept fresh in the fridge.

After slipping into her red lace lingerie, Ava felt a surge of confidence. The delicate fabric accentuated her curves, the lace pattern playfully teasing the eye. She added a touch of her favorite perfume, its scent as enticing as the lingerie. Standing before the mirror, Ava admired her reflection. The lingerie set off her skin tone beautifully, and her hair fell in soft waves around her shoulders.

She smiled, her eyes sparkling with mischief and anticipation. "Sexy night will be tonight!" she giggled to herself, amused and excited by her own playful words.

As she heard the front door open, Ava quickly positioned herself on the bed, her heart racing with excitement. She reclined gracefully, propped up on one elbow, her other hand resting lightly on her hip. This pose showcased the elegant lines of her figure, the red lace of her lingerie offering a striking contrast against the soft bedding.

Her legs were crossed at the ankles, adding an air of casual elegance. Ava's eyes sparkled with anticipation, her lips curved into an inviting smile. The dim candlelight in the room cast a warm glow over her, enhancing the romantic and intimate ambiance. She was the picture of allure, waiting for Ethan's reaction to her carefully planned surprise.

"Babe?" Ethan's voice echoed, tinged with surprise at the petal-strewn floor and the dimly lit room, illuminated only by candles. The scent of fresh perfume filled the air.

"I'm here!" Ava called out, adding a sultry tone to her voice. Ethan's sharp intake of breath upon entering the bedroom was the only sound for a moment.

"Babe? Don't you like how I look?" Ava asked, noting his stunned silence.

Ethan's laughter, soft and warm, dissolved the last traces of tension in the air. "Are you trying to seduce me, woman?" he asked, his voice a deep melody that resonated with affection and desire.

Ava's grin broadened, her eyes alight with a playful yet intense passion. She gave a slow, deliberate nod, her gaze locked with his. Ethan closed the distance between them with measured steps, each one charged with anticipation.

As he reached her, he gently cradled her face in his hands, his touch as tender as it was familiar. Ava's cheeks flushed with a rosy hue, her heart fluttering like a captive bird. Despite the countless times they had been this close, each touch from Ethan felt like a new discovery, a treasure unearthed.

"I've missed you, babe," she whispered, her voice barely above a breath. Her eyes, deep pools of emotion, conveyed more than words ever could. They reflected love, longing, and a yearning that had only grown during their time apart.

Ethan gazed into her eyes, finding himself lost in the depth of her emotions. He didn't respond with words; the moment called for a language beyond the spoken. Gently, he leaned in and captured her lips with his in a deep, affectionate kiss. It was a kiss that spoke of missed moments and rekindled flames, a kiss that seemed to stop time.

After weeks of missing each other due to Ethan's busy schedule, their embrace now deepened with a sense of urgency and familiarity. The dim candlelight cast a soft glow over them as they came together, reconnecting not just in heart but in body too. Laughter and whispers filled the room, a mix of relief and renewed passion.

Each touch and kiss was filled with all the love and longing they'd been holding back. It was clear they were making up for lost time, their actions speaking louder than any words could. The night turned into a rediscovery of each other, a reminder of their deep connection.

In the comfort of their shared space, Ava and Ethan let their love take physical form, rekindling the intimacy that had been put on hold. It was familiar yet filled with a new intensity, a celebration of their love and a reassertion of their bond.

This evening was about them being together in the most intimate way, reigniting the passion that was always there, just waiting for the right moment to come alive again.

CHAPTER FIVE

In the heart of her quaint shop, Ava called a meeting with her close friends - Amy, Carlson, Tony, and Jasmine. She had a sparkle in her eye and an excited tremor in her voice as she shared her plan for Ethan's surprise birthday party.

"Okay, everyone," Ava began, her eyes sparkling with enthusiasm. "Ethan's birthday is coming up, I've been brainstorming and I think I have the perfect idea," Ava began, her enthusiasm infectious. "I want to rent out this amazing rooftop venue I found. It has a stunning view of the city skyline, perfect for a memorable evening. We'll have a classy, elegant theme, with a live band playing Ethan's favorite music. I'm thinking of a night under the stars, where everything is about enjoying good food, great music, and the best of company."

Amy was the first to respond, her face lighting up. "Ava, that sounds incredible! Ethan will love it. And the rooftop setting? Absolutely perfect!"

Carlson nodded in agreement. "The view will definitely make it special. It's like something out of a movie."

Tony, with his usual enthusiasm, added, "Count me in for the distractions! Carlson and I will make sure Ethan has no idea what's coming. We'll come up with a convincing way to get him to the venue without suspecting a thing."

Jasmine, always attentive to detail, chimed in. "I can help with the decorations and setting up the place. We can make it look magical with the right lighting and decor."

Ava smiled, relieved and grateful for her friends' support. "Thank you, everyone! I knew I could count on you. Let's make this the best birthday Ethan has ever had!"

The group spent the next few hours discussing and refining the details, their excitement growing as the plan came together. It was a mix of great ideas, teamwork, and the shared joy of creating something special for Ethan. Ava felt a warm glow of happiness, knowing that with her friends by her side, the surprise party would be nothing short of spectacular.

Ethan was waiting outside Ava's shop, looking sharp in his winter gear. He wore a gray overcoat that was both stylish and practical for the cold, paired with a snug white sweater that made him look like he just stepped out of a winter fashion catalog. His scarf, a checkered pattern of dark and light grays, was draped casually around his neck, and he wore it like a natural accessory. The winter air seemed to highlight his striking features, making him stand out even more.

"Babe!" Ava couldn't hide her surprise and joy. She ran over and gave him a tight hug, feeling the warmth of his coat against the cold air. "This is a surprise!" Ethan's laugh was muffled by the scarf, a happy sound in the chilly evening.

"Got off early today and thought why not grab dinner with my favorite person?" he said with a smile. "It's cold out, and I bet you're starving."

Ava stepped back, beaming up at him. "Starving and freezing! You read my mind, Ethan."

They shared a quick, warm kiss before Ethan playfully nudged her towards his car. "Come on, I know just the place."

They strolled to his car, and Ethan held the door open for her, the gesture as warm as the kiss they shared before she got in. The drive to the Japanese restaurant was filled with their usual banter, discussions about mundane things like the latest series they were watching and Ethan's humorous anecdotes from the hospital.

As they sat in the warm glow of the restaurant, enjoying the array of sushi and sashimi, Ava remembered to lay the groundwork for her surprise. "You know, with all the appointments I've packed into next week, I almost let your birthday slip my mind," she said with a slight chuckle, hoping she sounded convincingly distracted. "With my schedule, I can only manage something low-key in the evening. How does that sound?"

Ethan nodded, swirling his ramen thoughtfully. "Low-key is good," he said, a little too quickly, and then added, "Honestly, just winding down with you would be great. No big celebrations needed."

Ava nodded, her secret grin safely tucked away behind her bowl. "Quiet dinner it is, then," she agreed, trying to match his casual tone.

Ethan smiled, but Ava caught a fleeting look of disappointment in his eyes—a look that vanished as quickly as it appeared.

She turned her attention back to her ramen, her mind racing with anticipation. When the weekend arrived, she knew the surprise she had planned would light up his world like the first snow lights up the winter sky.

It was a special day for Ethan, marking another year around the sun, and fortuitously, his work shift ended early. He and Ava had made plans to celebrate his birthday at 6 pm in a simple yet intimate manner. However, with a few spare hours before their meeting, Ethan decided to catch up with his buddies at a local bar. Mindful of his evening plans with Ava, they kept the drinking session lighter than usual. Amidst the casual ambiance, Ethan, Tony, and Carlson shared a few beers, toasting to another year of life's journey.

As they exited the bar, the afternoon sun casting long shadows on the street, Tony, with a mischievous twinkle in his eye, proposed an impromptu plan. "How about another round at a different spot?" he suggested, his voice laced with excitement.

Ethan glanced at his wristwatch, its hands inching towards the latter half of the afternoon. "Guys, I'm not sure about this. It's already past four, and I need to pick up Ava," he replied, a tinge of regret in his voice for having to decline.

A knowing look passed between Tony and Carlson, their eyes communicating a shared secret. Tony, with a persuasive grin, said, "You've got plenty of time, dude. Just an hour more, that's all we ask." His laughter was light, but there was an underlying earnestness in his tone.

Carlson chimed in, his face struggling to hide a brewing surprise. "Yeah, Ethan, come on. Just one more round. We promise, then you're free to go."

Ethan, feeling the pull of friendship and the unspoken promise of a special occasion, let out a resigned yet amiable sigh. "Alright, but just one," he agreed, his decision reflecting the warm bond he shared with his friends.

Their destination was The Aerie, a newly inaugurated edifice renowned for its luxurious top-floor room, which boasted a private balcony offering a panoramic view of the city - an idyllic setting for a memorable gathering.

Ethan's curiosity piqued about their choice of The Aerie, yet he refrained from questioning, trusting his friends' intentions. They ascended to the top floor, the elevator's smooth glide signifying their rise to an evening full of surprises.

Tony, leaning casually against the elevator wall, remarked, "You're going to love this place, Ethan. It's got the most lavish bar and the finest wines. Been wanting to check it out since it opened."

As they reached their destination, the anticipation in the air was palpable. The door to the exclusive room opened to reveal a heartwarming scene - a chorus of "Surprise!" filled the room, echoing with warmth and affection. There, gathered in the elegantly decorated space, were Ethan's closest - his family, friends, the Greenwood family, and most importantly, Ava, radiant in her chic cutout mini blazer dress and sleek black stilettos.

Ethan stood, momentarily stunned by the outpouring of love and affection, a genuine smile spreading across his face. "Happy birthday, Ethan!" the room resounded, a symphony of well-wishes and joyous exclamations.

Ava stepped forward, the embodiment of grace and affection. "Happy birthday, babe!" she repeated, her voice soft yet filled with excitement, as she planted a tender kiss on Ethan's cheek. "Were you surprised?"

His response came in a playful scoff, a blend of disbelief and heartfelt gratitude. "You really had me there. I honestly thought you were too busy to organize another surprise birthday party," he said, his voice tinged with admiration and surprise. As he spoke, his arms enveloped Ava in a warm, loving embrace, conveying the depth of his appreciation and affection.

Ava's smile was radiant, her eyes sparkling with the success of the surprise. "Anything for you, babe. Always," she said, her gaze briefly flickering towards Tony and Carlson, who were now reveling in Ethan's astonished reaction. "Thanks, you two," she added, acknowledging their crucial role in the surprise.

Tony's laughter was hearty and genuine. "Anything for a friend," he said, his eyes crinkling with mirth.

Carlson, joining in the laughter, added, "Happy to help, man. Enjoy your day!"

As the evening progressed, Ethan and Ava mingled with their guests, each interaction filled with laughter and stories, the room buzzing with the energy of a truly vibrant celebration.

The party was a lively affair, filled with the hum of music and the buzz of conversations. Ava mingled with her girlfriends, laughing and chatting away, while other guests enjoyed the wine and savored the catered delicacies.

Suddenly, Amy nudged Ava, a reminder lighting up her face. "Hey, Ava, I think it's time for the cake," she said, her voice a mix of excitement and gentle prompting.

"Oh, right," Ava laughed, a hint of embarrassment in her tone for almost forgetting the centerpiece of any birthday celebration – the cake. She scanned the room, looking for Ethan, but he was conspicuously absent. "Amy, could you guys get the cake ready? I'll go find the birthday boy," she asked, her voice tinged with a mix of urgency and amusement.

"Sure, of course," Amy replied, her enthusiasm for the upcoming cake-cutting evident.

"Thanks!" Ava said, her gratitude genuine. She then set off in search of Ethan, her eyes scanning the room. Spotting Carlson and some of the other guys engrossed in a game, she approached them. "Hey, guys. Have you seen Ethan? It's time for the birthday cake," she inquired, her voice carrying a note of playful impatience.

Carlson paused, scratching his head as he tried to recall. "Uhm, I think he was out on the balcony with Tony earlier, but that was like half an hour ago. Want me to go check?"

Ava offered a grateful smile. "No, it's alright. I'll check. Thank you," she replied, her tone appreciative.

Stepping out onto the balcony, Ava was greeted by a chilly breeze that made her hug herself for warmth. The balcony was deserted, likely due to the cold. However, the breathtaking view of the city skyline momentarily made her forget the chill in the air.

"It's so beautiful..." she whispered to herself, captivated by the panorama.

Just as she was about to head back inside, a voice caught her attention. It was coming from not too far off, and as she moved closer, the voice became more familiar – it was Tony's.

Curious, Ava edged closer, her footsteps quiet. She found Tony, cigarette in hand, deep in conversation with Ethan. They seemed engrossed in a serious discussion. As Ava drew nearer, intending to call out to Ethan, his words halted her in her tracks.

"I've never loved Ava. For the past seven years, I've never learned to love her," Ethan confessed, his voice heavy with an emotion she couldn't place.

Ava's breath hitched, her hand flying to her mouth in shock. Tears welled up in her eyes, each word from Ethan piercing her heart like shards of ice. She stood there, frozen, the joy of the evening shattered by the weight of his words.

CHAPTER SIX

Tony's voice rose in disbelief, echoing his shock at Ethan's confession. "What did you just say, Ethan?" he demanded, struggling to process the words.

Ethan, burdened with a heavy sigh, didn't reply. He simply took another sip of his beer. A short distance away, Ava stood frozen, absorbing every word her fiancé uttered.

"Six years, Ethan, not six days! You're saying you don't love her? That's impossible," Tony continued, frustration evident in his voice. "Is this about Violet again?"

Ethan inhaled sharply, the weight of his silence crushing. He nodded slowly, his gaze fixed on the ground, unable to face the truth in Tony's eyes.

"You can't let go of Violet, even after all this time?" Tony's voice rose, each word laced with incredulity and pain.

Ethan's voice, when it came, was a mere whisper, laden with unresolved grief. "Violet was my world, Tony. Then she disappeared, leaving nothing, not even a simple explanation... How does one move on from that?"

Ava's heart felt like it was being torn apart. She had never known about Ethan and Violet. The revelation was a chasm opening beneath her, swallowing her whole.

"And Ava... you used her to fill the void Violet left?" Tony's accusation was sharp, a knife cutting through the pretense. "Ava is our friend, Ethan. How could you play with her feelings like that?"

Ethan's voice trembled, every word laced with a confession of his deepest, most painful truth. "Tony, I swear, I tried to love her," he began, his voice cracking under the weight of his guilt. "But every time I told Ava 'I love you,' it felt like a lie clawing at my throat. Every kiss, every embrace... it was torture."

He paused, swallowing hard, his eyes reflecting a turmoil of emotions. "Waking up next to her, seeing Ava's face instead of Violet's... it was a daily nightmare, a reminder of what I'd lost and what I was pretending to have. I hated it, Tony. I hated the pretense, the charade of a love I couldn't feel."

Ethan's confession hung in the air, a stark, painful truth that cut through the silence. "Every 'I love you' only meant for Violet. I was living a lie, every single day, and it was killing me inside.

Ava felt as if the ground beneath her had given way, her world shattering into fragments with each of Ethan's words. His confessions tore through her heart, each sentence a brutal, unrelenting assault on her emotions. It was inconceivable to her - this person, uttering such heart-wrenching truths, couldn't be the Ethan she knew and adored.

In her mind, she clung desperately to the image of the Ethan she loved – the one who cherished her, who would never dream of inflicting such pain. She repeated it to herself, a mantra against the tide of despair, refusing to believe that the foundation of her life could crumble so cruelly, so suddenly.

But the reality was unyielding, and her tears flowed ceaselessly, each one a testament to the raw, overwhelming grief that engulfed her. The Ethan she thought she knew, the man she had entrusted her heart to, seemed now like an illusion, leaving her adrift in a sea of betrayal and heartache.

"For six years, I've been waiting, hoping Violet would come back. I planned to leave Ava then," Ethan added, his voice a hollow echo of his inner turmoil.

"Seriously, Ethan, this is messed up!" Tony's voice was filled with anger and disbelief. "If you feel like this, why haven't you ended things with Ava?"

Ethan looked deeply troubled. "I just... haven't found the right moment, and I don't know how to break it to her. I really don't want to hurt Ava, Tony. She's been nothing but wonderful to me." He buried his face in his hands, overwhelmed by guilt and regret.

"Do you have to end it with Ava? Are you really going to throw away six years over someone who's already left you?" Tony's probing questions sought a clear response.

Ethan responded firmly, "Yes, I have to break up with her. I'm just figuring out the right time."

Ava, her heart in ruins, stumbled away from her hiding spot. Her steps were shaky, her world spinning out of control. She needed to escape, to breathe, to find a way to stitch her broken heart back together. The night air was cold, but it was nothing compared to the icy grip of heartbreak clutching her soul.

As she re-entered the party, Amy approached her, eyes full of concern. "Ava, did you find Ethan?"

Ava choked back a sob, her world crumbling around her. "No, he's not outside," she managed to say, her voice a fragile thread. "Let's wait a bit longer."

Ava's tears were hidden behind a forced smile, but her heart was screaming, shattered by a truth too painful to bear.

Moments later, Ethan and Tony reentered the room, seemingly unperturbed by the earlier conversation. Ava hesitated, conflicted about approaching her fiancé; Ethan's hurtful words still echoed painfully in her mind. When his eyes found hers, she bit her lip, unsure how to mask her turmoil.

Jasmine's voice broke the tension. "Oh, finally the birthday boy is back! We've been waiting for you, dummy."

Ethan's laugh felt jarring to Ava. "Why?" he asked with feigned ignorance.

"It's time to blow out your birthday cake candles and make a wish!" Amy interjected cheerfully. "Ava, come over here! Ethan's back." Amy beckoned, and Ava, summoning every ounce of strength, stepped forward.

Tony and Carlson fetched the three-layered cake Ava had painstakingly baked. It was a stunning creation, each layer artfully adorned with delicate icing swirls and vibrant edible flowers, the top crowned with a shimmering 'Happy Birthday' topper. Ava stood by her parents, watching as her friends carefully placed the cake on the round table. But Ethan gently pulled her to his side, his grip firm yet tender.

As everyone sang 'Happy Birthday,' Ethan's hand held hers with a surprising intensity. Ava felt every eye on them, every note of the song amplifying her inner turmoil.

"Make a wish, son," Ethan's dad urged jovially.

Ethan turned to Ava, his gaze affectionate yet haunting. "Do I need to? I can't wish for anything more, now that I have you by my side," he declared, drawing cheers and playful jeers from their friends. Ava forced a smile, concealing the agony that Ethan's words inflicted.

After blowing out the candles and receiving a celebratory kiss on her head from Ethan, who whispered, "Thank you for this party, babe. I love you," Ava felt her heart fracture further. His caress, once tender, now felt like a cruel reminder of the truth she had overheard.

Unable to contain the flood of emotions, tears spilled down Ava's cheeks. Ethan's concern seemed genuine as he wiped them away, his touch inadvertently deepening her pain.

"Oh, baby, why are you crying?" His voice, soft and caring, was a stark contrast to his earlier confessions.

Ethan's mother cooed, "Aww, your fiancé clearly loves you so much, Ethan." The room filled with warm, affectionate murmurs, oblivious to Ava's internal struggle as Ethan held her, trying to comfort her.

It took a while, but Ava's tears eventually subsided. "I... I'm just overwhelmed with happiness being here with you..." she managed to say, her gaze locking with his. "I love you so much!" Her declaration was fervent, her embrace tighter than before, a desperate attempt to cling to a love that now felt as fragile as glass.

As Ava and Ethan embraced, the room hummed with the affectionate chatter of their friends and family. Gradually, attention shifted to the magnificent birthday cake that Ava had created. The guests marveled at its beauty, the intricate icing patterns and vibrant edible flowers drawing admiring comments.

"That cake is a work of art, Ava," one of the guests remarked, their eyes wide with appreciation.

"It's absolutely beautiful," another chimed in, "You've outdone yourself this time."

The atmosphere in the room was warm and convivial as everyone gathered around the table. Despite the turmoil within her, Ava managed to wear a gracious smile, accepting the compliments with a quiet thank you. The cutting of the cake became a communal event, with laughter and light conversation filling the air.

Ethan sliced the cake, his movements careful and considerate, each piece served to their friends and family a testament to

Ava's culinary skills. As the cake was passed around, the rich aroma and exquisite taste garnered further praise. Everyone ate together, the sweetness of the cake momentarily lightening the mood.

Ava watched the scene, a bittersweet feeling in her heart. The joy and camaraderie around her were a stark contrast to the storm of emotions raging within her. She took a small bite of the cake, its flavor a reminder of the love and effort she had poured into it, now shadowed by the revelations of the evening.

The party continued, with laughter and conversation weaving through the room. But for Ava, the laughter was a distant sound, the conversations a blur. Her heart, heavy with unspoken pain, beat out a rhythm of love and loss, even as she smiled and played the perfect hostess.

Ava and Ethan returned home together after the party, their footsteps echoing in the empty hallway. The apartment, once a symbol of their shared happiness, now felt like a stage set for a tragedy. Ava's mind was a whirlwind of emotions, replaying the snippets of conversation she had overheard between Ethan and Tony.

Inside, Ethan, unaware of the turmoil brewing in Ava, moved about with a casual ease. He soon succumbed to sleep's embrace, his breathing steady and deep. Ava watched him for a moment, her heart a battleground of love and hurt. She then quietly slipped away to the adjacent room.

This room, with its bare walls and minimal furnishings, offered Ava the solitude she desperately needed. As the door closed, her composure, maintained throughout the evening, began to crumble. Tears, hot and unrestrained, flooded her cheeks. She sank to the floor, her back against the cold, unyielding surface.

Her sobs were silent but intense, each one a physical manifestation of her heartache. The room, barely lit by the moonlight filtering through the window, became a cocoon for her grief. Ava wrapped her arms around herself, as if trying to hold together the pieces of her breaking heart.

The words she had overheard, Ethan and Tony's conversation, replayed in her mind. Each sentence was a confirmation of her deepest fears, each pause filled with unspoken implications. She felt as if her trust had been shattered, the pieces too sharp and scattered to gather.

Ava remained there for hours, lost in her sorrow, until exhaustion overcame her. In the stillness of the night, her tears eventually ceased, leaving her drained. As dawn's first light crept into the room, it found Ava asleep on the floor, her face still wet with tears, a poignant picture of someone broken by the revelations of the night.

Ava awoke the next morning, her headache a throbbing testament to the night's tears. Her eyes, swollen and red, stung with the remnants of her sorrow. As she glanced at the clock, she realized it was already past ten. Assuming Ethan had left for work, she stepped out of the room, only to be startled by his presence in the kitchen, his hands busy with washing dishes.

"Morning, sunshine," Ethan greeted without turning, his voice carrying a cheerfulness that felt jarring to Ava. He continued, "I made some egg omelet. Eat," he said, still focused on the dishes.

Ava stood frozen for a moment, a few inches from him. Her heart throbbed painfully, a stark reminder of the turmoil she was hiding. "I thought you already went to the hospital," she managed to say after a heavy silence.

"Oh, I will leave in a few minutes. My shift starts at eleven," Ethan replied with a grin, still oblivious to the storm raging within Ava. She nodded, her movements slow and heavy, as she walked towards the table.

The pain she had cried out the night before still lingered, an overwhelming shadow on her heart. She felt the tears threatening to surface again but controlled them just in time as Ethan sat across from her, observing her with a curious gaze.

"Why were you sleeping in the other room, babe? I woke up and you weren't in our bed," he asked, his brows furrowed in concern.

Ava glanced at him, her eyes a clear display of her inner agony. She responded in her mind, 'Because you said you hated waking up to me...' She avoided his gaze, looking down at her plate.

"Did you cry?" Ethan's voice was laced with worry. He reached out, but she was quick to grab her fork, feigning interest in her breakfast. Luckily, Ethan seemed not to notice her discomfort.

"Ye...yeah. Uhm, I couldn't sleep right away last night, so I decided to watch 'The Notebook' rerun in the other room, so I wouldn't wake you up. And you know me, I cry easily," Ava replied, her voice strained with a forced cheerfulness.

Ethan chuckled softly, his expression softening. "Oh, silly. I thought something bad happened," he said, relieved. Glancing at the clock, he quickly stood up. "I have to go now, babe. See you tonight, okay?"

As he leaned in for a kiss, Ava subtly turned her head, and his lips landed on her cheek instead. He didn't seem to notice the slight, and hurriedly left for work. The moment the door shut behind him, Ava's façade crumbled, and her tears, once again, began to fall freely. Alone in the kitchen, the reality of her heartache enveloped her, each sob a whisper of the pain she bore in silence.

CHAPTER SEVEN

Ava's life became a delicate balancing act, straining to uphold a façade of normalcy amidst a torrent of emotions. Nighttime brought its own challenges; sleep eluded her, replaced by the bitter comfort of wine, which she sipped alone, lost in thought.

She had once eagerly anticipated Ethan's return home each evening, but now she found herself withdrawing. There was a deep longing within her to be near him, yet the pain of his betrayal made it unbearable to face him. Their home, once a haven of shared joy and love, now felt hollow, echoing with the unspoken tensions between them.

Ava began a heartrending routine. Each night, as Ethan's footsteps approached their bedroom, she would feign sleep, her body still and her breathing measured. Lying there, she listened to the sounds of his movements, a silent reminder of the chasm that had opened between them.

Then, when she sensed that Ethan had drifted to sleep, Ava would allow herself to open her eyes. In the dim light, she would gaze at his sleeping form, tracing the familiar lines of his face with her eyes. In those quiet, solitary moments, she could almost imagine that he was still the loving fiancé she had once known, the man who had genuinely loved her. This illusion, fragile as it was, brought her a fleeting sense of peace.

But it was a bittersweet solace. As she watched him, tears would often well up in her eyes, silently streaming down her cheeks. The contrast between the Ethan who lay asleep before her and the Ethan who had confessed his true feelings was stark and painful. Each night, as she gazed at him, a part of her mourned for the love they had lost, for the future they might never have.

"I've missed you, Ethan," Ava whispered, her voice barely audible in the stillness of the night.

Startled, she nearly leaped off the bed as Ethan suddenly opened his eyes. Her heart raced, shock registering in her wide eyes. "I'm glad to know my fiancée misses me," Ethan said, a hint of hurt lacing his voice.

"Ethan! You're... you're awake?" Ava stammered, caught off guard.

He raised an eyebrow. "Yes, I am. So, please be honest with me, babe." His expression softened, concern evident in his eyes. "Why have you been avoiding me?" There was unmistakable hurt in his gaze.

Ava's eyes darted away; she wasn't prepared for this confrontation. "Uh, I... I need to use the restroom," she mumbled, attempting to escape the intensity of the moment. But Ethan was quicker, his hand reaching out to grasp hers, pulling her close until their bodies were just inches apart.

"Please stop avoiding me," he pleaded, his breath warm against her skin.

"I'm not," she lied, her voice a whisper.

Ethan scoffed lightly. "Babe, do you think I haven't noticed? You keep your distance, we barely talk, and when I'm home, you pretend to be asleep. Why?"

He gently lifted her chin, forcing her to meet his eyes. Ava saw the pain her actions had caused him, and it was too much. Tears began to cascade down her cheeks, revealing her inner turmoil.

'Are you actually planning to break up with me, Ethan? *Is it really true that you don't love me? Six years, and all this time I was living a lie. How did we end up here? When you said you loved me, I thought it was real. Every kiss we shared became the highlight of my days. But now, knowing you were thinking of someone else, it all feels like a cruel illusion.*'

Ava thought to herself, her heart heavy with this painful realization. As she intently looked into Ethan's eyes, she couldn't bring herself to voice these thoughts aloud. Instead, tears flowed freely, each one a silent testament to her shattered dreams and unspoken agony.

As tears streamed down her cheeks, Ava was the picture of heartbreak, yet Ethan was at a loss, clueless about the storm raging inside her. Ava, usually bright and cheerful, now seemed lost in sadness. The sparkle that once lit up her eyes had vanished, leaving a stark contrast to the joy he was accustomed to.

His eyes, filled with worry and confusion, searched her face for answers she wasn't ready to give. He held her close, hoping against hope that whatever pain she was enduring would soon fade away, replaced by the comfort and security of his embrace.

Amy playfully nudged Ava as they shared tea in her quaint shop. "Getting wedding jitters?" she teased. "Your big day is just a month away."

Ava managed a smile, her heart heavy with unspoken fears of the wedding being called off. "Not really. I'm just excited for the day to arrive. I can't wait to be Ethan's wife," she said, her heart swelling with a mix of hope and apprehension.

Amy's eyes twinkled mischievously. "Remember how you used to daydream about marrying Ethan back in college? Now it's actually happening. I'm so thrilled for you both."

A hint of nostalgia mixed with sorrow appeared on Ava's face as she thought back to her college days, when she was smitten with Ethan long before they became a couple. She recalled the countless times she daydreamed about being his wife.

A tear slipped from Ava's eye, and before she could wipe it away, Amy noticed. Her best friend's expression immediately filled with concern. "Ava, are you okay? You and Ethan didn't have a fight, did you? But that's unlikely; you two always get along so well."

Ava exhaled a deep sigh, torn about whether to confide in Amy. Since Ethan's birthday night, her heart had been burdened, and she longed to share her feelings, particularly with Amy. Yet, she found herself unable to speak the truth.

Attempting a smile, Ava reassured her, "No, Amy, Ethan and I are fine. Maybe you were right about me just having wedding jitters." She forced a light laugh, trying to mask her true emotions.

Amy studied Ava closely, searching for signs of truth in her response. "Okay, just remember, if something's on your mind, you can always talk to me," she said with a warm, reassuring smile, gently holding Ava's hand. "I'm here for you, no matter what."

Ava nodded, grateful. "Thank you, Amy."

Their conversation gradually shifted to lighter topics. Over a sip of tea, Amy casually asked, "So, about Fred's birthday - are we going together, or is Ethan picking you up?"

Ava replied, "Ethan mentioned he might be running late, so he suggested I go first. Can I catch a ride with you?" Deep down, Ava wasn't keen on going, but she couldn't find a plausible excuse to skip the event.

"Of course," Amy smiled warmly. "Any idea what Fred meant by 'a surprise' in his message? He's being so cryptic."

Ava chuckled. "Maybe he's getting married?" They shared a knowing look and burst into laughter, thinking of Fred, the perennial bachelor of their group.

It was a typical evening in the small town, the sky painted in hues of orange and pink as Ava and Amy left the boutique, chatting animatedly about their plans. They were heading to Fred's house, where a small, intimate birthday gathering was set to take place. Ava, despite her personal turmoil, was

THE ILLUSION OF US

looking forward to spending time with her close friends, a temporary escape from her own troubles.

Upon their arrival, they were greeted by the familiar, comforting scene of their friends gathered in Fred's cozy living room. Everyone was there, except for Ethan. Ava reassured everyone that he was held up at work but would join them later. The atmosphere was light and jovial, a stark contrast to Ava's hidden anxieties.

"So, Fred, about your text last night mentioning a surprise announcement?" Sofia inquired, her curiosity echoed by the others gathered in the living room.

"Yeah, what's this big news?" Tony added, equally intrigued.

Fred, pausing to take a sip of his beer, looked around at his friends. "Well, I had a talk with my dad last week. He's planning to retire and wants me to take over our family's architectural firm in Toronto. After giving it a lot of thought, I've decided to accept. So, I'm moving back to Canada next week," he explained, his tone casual despite the gravity of the decision.

"Next week?!" The group exclaimed in unison, visibly stunned by the suddenness of the news.

With a grin, Fred confirmed, "Yes, next week. So, tonight is not just a birthday celebration but also my farewell party."

Carlson and Tony, still processing the news, approached Fred. "Are you serious? This isn't a joke?" Tony asked, struggling to believe it.

"Fred, are you sure you've thought this through?" Carlson probed, concern evident in his voice.

"I have," Fred replied with conviction. "It's a big step, but I owe it to my dad. He's dedicated his life to building a better future for us, and now it's my turn to carry on his legacy."

The mood in the room shifted as Fred's friends absorbed the news, their initial shock giving way to a mix of sadness and support. Ava approached Fred, sincerity in her eyes. "If this is what makes you happy, Fred, then I'm happy for you." She embraced him warmly. "I'll miss you," she added, her voice tinged with emotion.

Fred returned the hug tightly. "Thanks, Ava," he whispered. "Remember, Canada's just an eight-hour drive away. You're all welcome to visit anytime." Despite the bittersweet nature of the announcement, the group rallied around Fred, offering their support and best wishes for his new venture.

As the evening progressed, Ava found herself increasingly immersed in the festivities. Fred, with a lighthearted chuckle, pointed out the empty beer cans accumulating beside her. "Wow, Ava. When did you become such a drinker?" he joked, eliciting curious glances from the others.

"Maybe it's because Ethan hasn't arrived yet?" Fred continued, his tone teasing but not without a hint of concern.

Ava, maintaining her composure, laughed along. "I'm just enjoying the moment with my dear friends," she replied, her smile not quite reaching her eyes.

The conversation soon turned nostalgic, with Tony chiming in, "Old friends, you mean. We're not that old!" His comment broke the momentary tension, and laughter filled the room once again.

Amy, with a knowing look, added, "Remember how Ava used to outdrink all of us in college? Even you, Fred, couldn't keep up with her!"

Carlson, after taking a sip from his beer, reminisced, "Those were the days when everyone would be tipsy, but Ava would still be standing tall, no matter how many beers she had."

Ava feigned offense. "Are you implying I'm an alcoholic?"

"No, just that you loved partying hard," Amy teased, playfully pinching Ava's cheeks.

Fred joined in, a hint of nostalgia in his voice. "Yeah, until you started dating Ethan." Ava sensed a fleeting sadness in his tone, but it quickly vanished.

As time ticked by, Tony, glancing at his watch, raised a valid concern. "It's already 7 pm. Isn't Ethan coming?" He looked at Ava, who seemed increasingly uneasy.

Ava nodded, a hint of worry in her voice. "I tried calling him, but no answer. His shift should have ended by now. Let me try again." Excusing herself, she stepped away to call Ethan. The phone rang and rang, but there was no answer. Ava's worry intensified. She decided to call George, Ethan's coworker and a fellow resident at the hospital.

"Hey, Ava. What's up?" George's voice was casual, unaware of Ava's growing anxiety.

"George, is Ethan still at the hospital? I can't reach him," Ava asked, her voice tinged with worry.

George's response did little to calm her nerves. "He left early, like two hours ago. I thought he was with you."

Ava's heart pounded erratically with fear. "No, he's not here. Thanks, George. I'll keep trying to call him." Ending the call, Ava's mind raced with possibilities. She considered sharing her concerns with the group but was interrupted by the sound of a car pulling up in the driveway.

Relief flooded her when she recognized Ethan's car. She rushed to greet him, eager for a reassuring hug, but froze in shock when the door opened to reveal Ethan... with Violet.

CHAPTER EIGHT

"Violet..." Ava murmured, her gaze oscillating between Ethan and Violet. Observing them together, memories of Ethan and Violet as a couple flooded her mind.

"Babe?" He called out, but Ava's attention was riveted on Violet. Ethan, following her gaze, also looked at Violet. "Sorry I'm late," he stammered, moving towards Ava.

Then Violet interrupted, exclaiming as she enveloped Ava in a hug, "Ava, it's been ages!"

Ava, rigid in Violet's embrace, clenched her fist secretly. "Violet, you're back?" Her eyes met Ethan's, detecting a flicker of guilt before he averted his gaze.

"Yep, I've returned!" Violet beamed, stepping back from the hug.

The sound of Fred's voice approached from the living room, accompanied by their friends. They all appeared startled upon seeing Violet.

"Hi everyone, I'm back!" Violet greeted, waving enthusiastically. However, the group's response was tepid, their faces etched with confusion and concern, particularly towards Ava. It was as if they all knew about Ethan and Violet's past relationship.

Amy, with a tone of displeasure, queried, "Ethan, did you pick Violet up from the airport? Why did you arrive together?" Her question echoed Ava's unspoken thoughts.

Ethan finally approached Ava, his steps heavy with reluctance. "Hi, love, sorry I'm late," he murmured, meeting her eyes. "I... uh..."

"Can't you all show a little excitement to see me?" Violet interjected, feigning disappointment. "I wanted it to be a surprise! I lost your numbers but still had Ethan's, so I asked him for a lift from the airport. I knew you'd all be here for Fred's birthday." She leaned in to peck Fred on the cheek. "Happy birthday, Fred!"

Ava noticed the others' disdainful scoffs. Violet, glancing at Ava, said, "I assumed Ethan told you, Ava. I didn't think you'd keep secrets, especially with your wedding coming up." Her smirk was thinly veiled.

A chill ran through Ava, but she masked her pain with a smile, wrapping her arms around Ethan's waist. "You should've mentioned Violet's return, Ethan. We could have prepared a proper welcome," she said, kissing him.

Ethan replied awkwardly, "I'm sorry..."

Tony intervened, easing the tension by ushering everyone back to the dining room. Ethan and Ava sat together, with Violet directly opposite them.

"As we were saying, time to sing 'Happy Birthday' to Fred and enjoy the cake," Sofia chimed in. Carlson emerged with the birthday cake.

Following the birthday song, Fred thanked Ava for the cake. "It's gorgeous," he praised.

"Of course," Ava replied, her smile hiding the turmoil within.

Laughter and stories flowed as freely as the wine, with the group reminiscing about everything from Fred's relocation to Canada to the upcoming wedding. Ava watched her friends, a content smile on her face as she cut the cake she had baked herself.

However, the mood shifted when Violet, with a hint of mischief in her smile, said, "So, Ava, did you know that Ethan and I used to date in college just right before I left for France?" Her tone was casual, but it carried an undercurrent of something more.

The room fell silent, and their friends exchanged startled glances. Violet continued, glancing at Ethan, "We dated for uh..." She paused expectantly. "How long was it again, Ethan?"

Ethan, caught off guard, stammered, "H...huh?"

Violet flicked her fingers dismissively. "Right, we dated for two years. Almost three."

Amy, Sofia, and Jasmine rolled their eyes in unison, visibly annoyed. Amy's voice, sharp with irritation, cut through the tension. "It's in the past now, Vi. It's irrelevant. Why bring it up?"

Unfazed, Violet turned to Ava. "I just wanted to ask if you knew. We were each other's first love, after all. And I wanted to let you know, Ava, that there's no hard feelings."

Ava clenched her fists under the table, her heart racing. "Of course, I knew," she lied, her voice steady but her insides churning. "If you hadn't left six years ago, you and my fiancé might have been married by now." Her words were bold, yet they echoed painfully in her heart.

Violet's smile wavered, and Ava felt a momentary sense of triumph.

Violet raised her beer can, attempting to lighten the atmosphere. "Oh well, just like what Amy said, it's all in the past now. I'm happy for both of you. So, cheers!" The toast was echoed, though the cheerfulness was somewhat strained.

Ethan, looking visibly upset, suddenly stood up. "I'm just gonna get some fresh air," he muttered, then walked out. Ava was left hanging, a wave of concern washing over her.

The boys, sensing the tension, followed Ethan out. The girls remained at the table, each lost in their thoughts. Ava decided to help Fred with the cleanup, giving Ethan the space he needed.

In the kitchen, Ava silently cleared the plates and loaded the dishwasher, her mind a whirlwind of emotions. Fred returned from taking out the trash and noticed her preoccupied look. "Are you okay in here, Ava?" he asked, concern etched in his voice. "I'm sorry I made you clean up."

She chuckled, a sound more forced than amused. "No worries. I don't mind at all." They leaned against the countertop, waiting for the dishwasher to finish, their friends' muted voices drifting in from the patio.

Fred hesitated before speaking again. "I wanted to know if you're alright. Violet's words earlier were quite surprising."

Ava smiled, but it was tinged with bitterness. "I'm good. Thanks for asking, Fred. Did you know too that they dated before?"

Fred nodded. "I was surprised to know that you knew as well. They only dated secretly. We found out about it a few months before Vi left for France." He looked at her curiously. "How did you know?"

Ava's smile faded, her heart heavy. "Two weeks ago..." she confessed softly.

Fred saw the pain in her eyes and tried to offer comfort. "But hey, you're the one he's getting married to. Don't let their past relationship affect you, okay? You're the one he's in love with."

Ava's heart sank further. *'He's not in love with me'*, she wanted to confess, but the words wouldn't come. Her eyes welled up, meeting Fred's gaze filled with concern.

As the evening came to a close, with Amy and Carlson announcing their departure, Ava remained in a daze. "Where's Ethan?" she asked, her voice laced with worry.

"He went back to the balcony upstairs," Carlson informed her.

Ava dashed upstairs, needing to tell Ethan that Carlson and Amy were leaving. As she hit the top step, she spotted Ethan on the balcony, beer in hand. She almost approached him, but then Violet showed up next to him. Ava ducked out of sight, shocked to see Violet there. They seemed so close, too close.

Violet broke the silence. "I thought you'd wait for me," she said, a mix of surprise and hurt in her voice. Ethan, caught off guard, just looked at her. "You kept texting, asking me to come back, even though you weren't sure I'd get the messages. So why are you getting married now?" Violet asked, sounding betrayed.

Ethan, lost for words, just took another sip of his beer. "You said you loved me. Was that just to get me back here?"

He replied, troubled, "When I said I loved you, I meant it."

Violet's voice was full of disappointment. "Then why go through with the wedding? You knew I was coming back. I thought you'd have broken it off with Ava."

Ethan ran his hand through his hair, clearly frustrated. "Ava and I have been together six years. I can't just throw her away. You should get that, Violet, after all you've put me through."

Violet's face showed guilt. "Your dad wanted me out of the picture. He threatened my future. I had to leave you for my family's sake."

Violet stepped back, crying. "He would have ruined my chance to become a doctor, and I needed that to help my family out of poverty. I've always told you about this. Leaving you tore me apart. But now, I'm back, on my own terms. Ethan, please, come back to me. I can't stand seeing you with her."

Ethan's face softened, and he held her close. "I promise, I will," he whispered, their eyes locked in a silent promise.

Ava, hidden from view, felt her heart break. There was Ethan, her fiancé, in the arms of another woman. She curled up, trying to comfort herself. Luckily, their friends were too busy downstairs to notice her breaking down.

Ava's tears were a silent river, flowing unnoticed until Amy found her, concern etched on her face. Ava, with a trembling voice, begged Amy not to cause a scene. They quietly moved to the back of the house, a quiet spot away from the drama.

"Ava, he's your fiancé! You can't just let this slide," Amy insisted, anger and a desperate need to protect Ava in her voice.

Ava's smile was a cracked facade. "Confront them? For what? It's painfully obvious Ethan was never really mine." Her voice broke, and the floodgates opened. She collapsed into Amy's arms, her body wracked with sobs, each one a testament to the depth of her heartache.

"He... he said he never loved me," Ava sobbed, her voice breaking. "All this time, Ethan was just pretending. It's like I'm trapped in a nightmare I can't escape, Ames. It hurts so bad!"

"What are you gonna do now, Ava?" Amy asked, her voice a mix of worry and determination. "You're not gonna just let him go, right? Fight for him, for you guys..."

Ava's voice was shaky, filled with doubt. "I don't know, Ames. Does Ethan even want me to fight for him?" Her eyes were swimming in tears. "I've loved him my whole life. But he's in love with Vi. How do I make him stay when he's set on someone else?" Her sobs were quiet but heart-wrenching.

Amy was firm, almost insistent. "Come on, Ava. Six years is a long time. There's no way Ethan felt nothing all those years. Perhaps Ethan's just tangled in past memories because Vi's back. But don't throw in the towel just yet. Trust what you guys had, it's gotta count for something."

Ava's tears slowed down, Amy's words sinking in. A tiny spark of hope flickered in her. "You're right. I can't just give up. I've got to fight for us." Amy's words lit a fire in Ava, reviving her fighting spirit.

"That's my girl. Now, go get your man upstairs. We'll head out together," Amy encouraged, a proud smile on her face. She gently tucked Ava's hair behind her ear. Together, they walked back inside. Ava, with newfound resolve, went upstairs to fetch Ethan.

Violet's expression turned to stone as Ava told Ethan she wanted to leave. Ethan hesitated, a conflict visible in his eyes, but ultimately, he had no choice but to follow his fiancée.

Hand in hand, Ava and Ethan left Fred's house, joined by Amy and Carlson. Sofia and Jasmine, meanwhile, offered to drive Violet back to her hotel.

Ethan's silence during the drive was deafening, his face a mask of seriousness that left Ava too intimidated to break the silence. Upon arriving at their apartment, he brushed past her, his silence like a wall between them.

"Babe, what's wrong?" Ava ventured, her voice trembling, even though she knew the answer. He was upset about leaving Violet behind, and now his mood was heavy and sullen. She approached him, her hands gently caressing his arms. "You look so tired. How about a warm bath to relax?" Her smile was full of love, but her heart was heavy.

Ethan's gaze lingered on her, distant and pained, as if he was seeing someone else in her place. Ava's heart twisted painfully at the thought, and she quickly looked away.

"I'll get your bath ready," she murmured, not waiting for his reply. In the bathroom, as the water filled the tub, Ava crumpled to the floor, her whole body wracked with sobs that she tried to stifle with her hands over her mouth.

The vivid image of Ethan and Violet, intimately close, replayed in her mind like a cruel loop, each scene slicing through her heart. The pain was raw and consuming, tearing through her with a ferocity that left her feeling utterly exposed and vulnerable. In that moment, alone on the cold bathroom floor, Ava felt the full weight of her heartbreak, a deep, aching emptiness that seemed to echo through her entire being.

After a while, a knock at the door jolted her. "Ava, are you okay in there?" Ethan's voice, laced with concern, barely reached her.

"Ye...yeah. Just a minute," she called out, barely recognizing her own voice. Rising to the sink, her reflection in the mirror was that of someone shattered, a shadow of her usual self. She washed her face, erasing the tear streaks, and forced a bright smile.

Opening the door, she said cheerfully, "The bath's ready for you."

"Thanks, babe," Ethan replied, his voice empty. As he began to close the door, Ava stopped him, gripping the doorknob. "Need anything else?"

"Join you in the bath?" she offered playfully, attempting to lighten the mood. Ethan did smile, but it was hollow, not reaching his eyes.

"Maybe next time, babe. I'm just too tired today," he said, his expression blank as he closed the door on her. Ava stood there, her hand still on the doorknob, feeling more alone than ever.

Ava slipped into her pajamas and laid out Ethan's on the closet drawer. Settling into bed, she opened a book, trying to distract herself while waiting for Ethan to finish his bath. As time ticked by, her eyelids grew heavy, but her attention snapped to Ethan's phone lighting up and vibrating on the bedside table. It was Violet calling.

Tempted to answer, Ava hesitated as the bathroom door creaked open. Quickly, she lay back down, feigning sleep. Ethan's footsteps approached the bed.

"Hello? Yeah, sorry we had to rush off," Ethan spoke, his voice even. "You got to your hotel okay? Good," she heard him say. He continued talking as he changed into his pajamas from the drawer.

The room fell silent for a few moments before Ethan picked up his phone again. "Yes, she's asleep," he murmured, continuing his conversation with Violet. Ava strained to hear more, but Ethan stepped out onto the balcony, closing the sliding door behind him.

Left alone in the bed, Ava could feel the distance between them widen with each passing minute as Ethan lingered on the balcony, engrossed in his talk with Violet. The bed felt emptier, colder, and Ava lay there, engulfed in a profound sense of isolation.

CHAPTER NINE

Ava lay sprawled on the sofa, her eyes repeatedly drifting to the clock as it inched towards two in the morning. The living room, dimly lit by a soft lamp, seemed to accentuate her growing unease. This had become her nightly ritual, waiting, as Ethan's recent pattern of coming home late gnawed at her. Each tick of the clock seemed to echo in the emptiness of the room, deepening the pit in her stomach, her mind tormented with thoughts of where Ethan might be.

The sound of a key in the lock snapped her out of her anxious reverie. Ethan stepped in, his footsteps resounding in the quiet room. Ava, her heart racing, sat up, attempting to cloak her worry with feigned nonchalance.

"Hey, you're late," she said softly, her voice laced with a weariness born of many such nights. "Was there an emergency at the hospital? Or maybe a last-minute surgery?"

Ethan, shrugging off his coat without meeting her gaze, replied casually, "Yeah, it was hectic. We had an unexpected situation in the ER. Just didn't stop all night."

Ava felt her heart sink. She knew he had left work hours ago, yet she desperately clung to the hope that her fears were unfounded. "That sounds intense. Must've been a really long night," she responded, struggling to keep her voice steady.

Ethan nodded, still avoiding her eyes. "It was. I'm beat. Sorry I didn't call, it was just non-stop."

A sharp pain gripped Ava's chest, her friend's earlier call echoing in her mind. They had seen Ethan and Violet together at the hotel where Violet was staying. She forced a smile, her hands clenched in her lap to hide her inner turmoil.

"I understand. You must be really exhausted," she said, her voice strained. "Do you need anything? Maybe something to eat, or a hot shower first?"

"No, I'll just head straight to bed. Thanks though," Ethan replied, his voice and demeanor distant, devoid of the warmth she longed for.

As he walked towards their bedroom, Ava was left alone on the sofa, the weight of his unspoken betrayal crushing her. She knew where he had been, and it wasn't at the hospital. The ease of his lies, the widening gap between them, it all overwhelmed her like a suffocating wave, leaving her submerged in a sea of heartache.

Ava was just about to drift off to sleep when the sudden light from Ethan's phone jolted her awake. Violet's name glared accusingly from the screen. Ava's first instinct was to ignore it, but the phone kept ringing insistently, and Ethan was fast asleep, oblivious.

Finally, with a mix of curiosity and a sinking feeling in her stomach, Ava picked up. "Ethan? Sorry, did I wake you?" Violet's voice was soft, almost cautious. "Ethan, are you there? Why aren't you talking?"

Ava stayed silent, her heart pounding in her chest.

"Oh, is Ava with you? That's okay, just listen then," Violet sighed, a hint of drama in her tone.

Then came the words that felt like a punch to Ava's gut. "I'm so happy we get to see each other every day, even if it's just for a little while. It reminds me of our college days, when we dated in secret because your dad didn't approve. I should never have left you because of him."

Ava's hand clutched at her chest, her breath catching in her throat.

Violet continued, now with a tearful edge to her voice. "I had no choice back then. Your dad threatened my scholarship, my future. But I regret it every day. Knowing you've forgiven me means the world to me, Ethan. You are my world."

Ava could barely breathe, the room spinning around her.

"And I know you're just waiting for the right time to break it off with Ava. I don't want to pressure you, but we've already lost six years. I can't lose any more time without you. Please, Ethan, leave Ava. Don't marry her. I love you, and I know deep down, you still love me."

Ava's tears flowed uncontrollably. Hearing Violet talk about spending time with Ethan every day, a secret they were

THE ILLUSION OF US

keeping from her, shattered her heart into a million pieces. She was living a lie, and it was crumbling before her very eyes.

In a daze of pain and betrayal, Ava ended the call without a word. She stumbled into the bathroom, locking herself in. There, alone with her heartache, she cried like she never had before. Her sobs were raw, filled with the agony of a love betrayed and a trust broken. She felt lost, utterly alone, her dreams and hopes for the future with Ethan dissolving into nothingness.

The next morning, Ava carried a tray of breakfast to Ethan, hoping to start the day on a positive note. It was his day off, and she had plans for them to spend quality time together, including a trip to the fifth avenue to buy a farewell gift for Fred, who was leaving for Canada.

"Hey, sleepyhead. Wake up..." Ava cooed, gently nudging Ethan awake. He grunted, still wrapped in sleep. She affectionately caressed his face and kissed his shoulder. "Wake up, love. It's getting late in the morning." Her grin was hopeful.

Her heart fluttered when Ethan responded with a genuine smile, something she hadn't seen in days. Propping himself up against the headboard, he eyed the breakfast - croissants, strawberry crepes with chocolate syrup, and freshly brewed coffee. "This looks scrumptious..." he murmured, his stomach audibly agreeing.

Ava's spirits lifted as she watched him enjoy the breakfast she'd prepared. "You should get ready after eating, babe.

We've got an hour before heading to go shopping" she reminded him cheerfully.

Ethan paused, his expression changing. "Uhm, babe, I can't go today. I swapped shifts with George; he had a family emergency in Wisconsin," he explained, sounding apologetic.

Ava's heart sank, her smile faltering. "Oh, is that so?" she sighed, her disappointment clear.

"I'm sorry," he added, looking somewhat uneasy.

"It's okay, I understand. Maybe next time. Just finish your breakfast, so you're not late for work," Ava said, managing a half-smile. She stood up and went to their closet to pick out his work clothes.

As she sorted through his clothes, Ava tried to sound upbeat. "Don't forget, next weekend is our bachelor and bachelorette party in Breckenridge. Amy and Tony have everything planned out."

Their friends had decided to celebrate Ethan's bachelor party and Ava's bridal shower simultaneously at a ski resort in Breckenridge, Colorado.

"Why do we have to go that far? We could have the party right here in New York," Ethan remarked, his tone lacking enthusiasm.

Ava turned to him, trying to hide her hurt. "We wanted something different, a change of scenery. It's a once-in-a-lifetime event, babe. I want it to be special," she insisted, still smiling.

Ethan just shrugged, showing little interest. Ava felt a sting of hurt but chose not to dwell on it. After finishing his breakfast, Ethan quickly headed to the bathroom to shower and get ready for work, leaving Ava alone with her thoughts, the distance between them growing more palpable by the day.

Ava wandered along Fifth Avenue, weaving through the array of stores. After much deliberation, she finally settled on a limited collection of ties from Hermès for Fred's farewell gift. On her drive home, she passed Ethan's favorite Chinese restaurant and decided to surprise him and his colleagues at the hospital with an assortment of dim sum platters.

She tried calling Ethan to let him know about her plan, but her calls went unanswered. Upon reaching the hospital, Ava made her way directly to the residents' lounge. She was a familiar face there – known both as the chairman's daughter and Ethan's fiancée – and was greeted warmly by the staff.

Entering the lounge, Ava was taken aback to find George there. "Hey, Ava. Good to see you," George greeted her cheerfully.

"H...Hi, George," Ava replied, managing a warm smile despite the confusion swirling in her mind. Ethan had mentioned swapping shifts with George, so what was he doing here? She wondered. Trying to maintain her composure, she asked, "Is Ethan in surgery, by any chance?" as she set down the bags of dim sum.

George looked puzzled. "It's Ethan's day off today. Shouldn't he be at home?" he said with a light chuckle, assuming she had simply mixed up the days.

Realizing the inconsistency in Ethan's story, Ava forced a laugh. "Ah, right. How silly of me to forget," she said, her voice tinged with feigned nonchalance. "Anyway, I brought some dim sum for everyone. Enjoy. I need to get going now. Thanks, George." She quickly left the room, her heart racing and mind reeling from the unexpected revelation.

Ava's heart felt heavy as she left the hospital, her mind swirling with confusion and hurt. Ethan had told her he swapped his day off with George, yet there was George, clearly not on an emergency trip to Wisconsin. The pieces didn't add up, and a sinking feeling settled in her stomach.

As she got into her car, she dialed Ethan's number again, her fingers trembling slightly with a mix of anxiety and hope. But again, there was no answer. "Where are you, Ethan?" she whispered to herself, the words barely audible, as she stared blankly at her phone.

In the back of her mind, a small, nagging voice suggested a possibility she didn't want to consider. But she pushed the thought away, not ready to confront the implications.

Ava found herself, almost without realizing it, parked outside Violet's hotel. She sat there for several moments, wrestling with the decision to go inside. Eventually, her need for the truth outweighed her hesitation. As she approached the hotel's entrance, her heart sank. Through the lounge window, she spotted Ethan. He was there, relaxed, sipping coffee. And beside him was Violet, laughing at something he had said.

The scene before her confirmed her worst fears. Ava had suspected they were seeing each other ever since Violet returned, but witnessing it firsthand was a different kind of agony. They looked so comfortable, so in sync, as if they were trying to make up for all the time they had lost. To Ava, watching from afar, they appeared every bit the couple, and she felt like the outsider.

'You really love her, don't you, Ethan?' she thought, her gaze fixed on them. Her heart felt like it was being torn apart as Violet reached out and tenderly held Ethan's hand on the table. He responded with a smile, a look of affection Ava hadn't seen directed at her for a long time. It was a smile she used to believe was reserved just for her, now shared with someone else – the person he truly loved.

Ava stood there, a silent witness to the scene, her heart breaking in silence. The realization hit her hard – the smile she cherished, the love she thought was hers, was now a distant memory, fading in the shadow of this new, painful reality.

Ava remained rooted to the spot, phone trembling in her hand as she watched Ethan from a heart-wrenching distance. When she called, her heart was a chaotic mix of hope and dread, half-expecting him not to answer. Yet, he did.

"Hey..." Ethan's voice, devoid of warmth, filtered through the phone.

"B...babe, where are you?" Ava's voice quivered, her grip on the phone tightening. Through the hotel's window, she could see Violet, curious and questioning, but Ethan gave nothing away. "Are you still at the hospital?" she asked, a faint hope for honesty flickering within her.

"Yeah, just finished assisting my attending with an aortic valve replacement," Ethan replied, his voice smooth, betraying no sign of the lie. Ava's heart dropped, a silent gasp escaping her lips as tears began to blur her vision. The reality of his deceit sliced through her. "Are you home?" he asked.

"Hmm," she managed to nod, though he couldn't see. "Babe?" Ava's voice was barely a whisper, a shattered echo of what it once was.

"Yeah? What is it?" Ethan's response was guarded, cautious.

"Have you seen Vi lately?" Ava asked abruptly, her heart racing as she waited for his reaction.

Ethan paused, a moment of hesitation that spoke volumes. Ava watched, her heart sinking, as he glanced briefly at Violet. "Uhm, no. Why?" he replied, feigning ignorance.

Ava's breath hitched, her efforts to sound casual crumbling. "I just thought... maybe we could invite her next week, in case Amy forgot. You'll tell me when you see her, right?" Her voice broke, betraying the turmoil within.

"Sure, but I doubt I'll see her. Maybe we should call her later?" Ethan suggested, his tone uneasy, distant.

"Okay. Later then," Ava replied, her voice hollow. "I love you, babe."

Ethan hesitated, his eyes darting between Violet and his phone, a silent battle raging within him. "Ethan?" Ava's voice was a faint echo of hope.

"Uhm, me too. See you later, okay?" His words felt like a final blow, distant and disconnected, before he abruptly ended the call. She stood there, frozen, as the reality of the moment crashed over her like a wave.

Through the glass, she could see Ethan's conflicted expression as he glanced between Violet and his phone, his hesitation cutting through her. When he finally muttered a half-hearted "me too" before abruptly ending the call, it was like a dagger to Ava's heart.

The silence that followed was deafening. Ava's hand trembled as she lowered the phone, tears streaming down her face. She watched as Ethan turned back to Violet, his smile returning, their laughter resuming as if nothing had happened. It was a stark, painful contrast to the despair engulfing her.

Ava felt a profound sense of betrayal, not just from the lies but from the realization that the man she loved, the man she was about to marry, was sharing moments with someone else that were meant for her. Each laugh, each tender glance that she witnessed was a reminder of what she had lost, of the future they would never have.

Her heart felt like it was being torn apart, each beat a reminder of the love she still felt for Ethan, a love that was now laced with pain and loss. She stood there, watching them, feeling more alone than ever before. The dream of their life together, once so vivid and full of promise, was now fading, leaving her in a world that suddenly felt cold and unrecognizable.

Ava turned away, her steps heavy as she walked back to her car. The world around her seemed to blur, her mind consumed by the heartbreak and the crushing weight of the truth she had just uncovered. She felt lost, adrift in a sea of emotions, with the painful realization that the man she loved had chosen someone else.

CHAPTER TEN

In the waning light of the evening, Ava, with a heart heavy as stone, bypassed the familiar route to her home. Instead, she found herself steering towards a nondescript bar, a place where the shadows of her life wouldn't find her. It was a quiet spot, unfamiliar and unremarkable, far from the eyes of those who knew her.

With a resolve that masked her inner turmoil, she approached the bar and ordered a shot of vodka, her voice barely above a whisper. The bartender, sensing her distress, served her quickly. Ava held the glass, its contents shimmering under the dim lights, like a fragile hope in the midst of her despair.

As she took the shot, her hand trembled, and the liquid fire did nothing to warm the chill in her heart. She ordered another, then another, each one a futile attempt to drown the agony that gnawed at her soul.

Ava's gaze drifted to her phone, to a wallpaper that now felt like a cruel reminder of a happier time. It was a photo of her and Ethan, radiant with joy on the day of his med-school graduation. Their smiles, so full of promise and dreams, now seemed to mock her current misery. She remembered the unspoken vows she made that day, to love and cherish him for a lifetime. Those dreams now lay shattered, like glass under the harsh truth of reality.

Tears, unbidden, cascaded down her cheeks. She tried to stifle her sobs, her body shaking with each wave of sorrow. "Why, Ethan? Why did you let me believe in a love that never was?" Her heart ached with the betrayal, the pain so raw and overwhelming that it felt physical.

More vodka came, but it tasted like ash in her mouth, each sip a bitter reminder of her shattered illusions. The alcohol, rather than numbing her pain, seemed to amplify it, each shot a piercing reminder of her loneliness.

Through her blurred vision, she caught a glimpse of the bartender's name tag. "Brian, can I have another?" Her voice was a broken whisper, the words barely escaping her lips.

Brian, the bartender, looked at her with a mix of pity and concern. "Miss, I think you've had enough," he said gently, his voice a soothing balm to her frayed nerves.

Ava's response was a choked laugh, devoid of any humor. "Enough? My heart is breaking, and you tell me I've had enough?" Her tears flowed freely now, each drop a testament to her shattered dreams.

"I thought he loved me, Brian. For six years, I believed we were building a life together. And now? He's gone, back to the arms of his past, leaving me here in pieces. How do I move on from that? How do I breathe knowing that every 'I love you' was a lie?"

Brian remained silent, offering her a glass of water, a small act of kindness in her world of pain. Ava looked at it, then back at him, her eyes pools of despair. "Water won't mend a broken heart, Brian. Nothing will."

She continued, her voice a haunting melody of pain and betrayal. "Do you know what it's like, Brian? To wake up one day and realize that the person you loved more than life itself never truly loved you back? That you were just a placeholder until their real love returned?"

Ava's sobs filled the quiet bar, her pain echoing off the walls. Brian listened, a silent witness to her heartbreak, his presence a small comfort in her world of hurt.

In that moment, Ava's grief was palpable, a raw, open wound for anyone to see. Her tears were a river of sorrow, her cries a lament for a love lost, a dream shattered. It was a scene of pure emotional devastation, a heart laid bare in its most vulnerable state.

It was just after eight in the evening when Ethan decided to head back home. The apartment greeted him with darkness and an unsettling silence.

"Babe?" He called out, flipping the light switch. There was no response. A quick check around the apartment confirmed that Ava wasn't there. Ethan found this odd; he had assumed Ava would be home by now. It was an unusual feeling for him, coming home to an empty apartment for the first time since they moved in together.

Concerned, Ethan pulled out his phone and dialed Ava's number. To his surprise, a man's voice answered. Ethan double-checked the screen to ensure he hadn't dialed the wrong number. It was definitely Ava's.

"Who's this?" Ethan asked, his voice edged with confusion and concern. "Where's Ava? I mean the owner of this phone?" The man on the other end quickly explained the situation and informed him of Ava's whereabouts. "Okay, I'll be right there," Ethan replied, a sense of urgency in his voice. He ended the call and rushed out, driving straight to the bar.

Upon entering the bar, Ethan immediately spotted Ava. She was slumped over the counter, evidently asleep on her barstool. Ethan had never seen her like this before; the sight fueled his worry that something serious was amiss.

Gently brushing the hair from her face, he noticed her flushed cheeks. "Babe?" he whispered, rubbing her back to wake her up.

"Here's her phone," said the bartender, handing it over but eyeing Ethan with an intense, almost scrutinizing gaze.

"How much did she drink? She looks really out of it," Ethan asked, his concern growing.

"Your girlfriend had ten shots of vodka before she passed out," the bartender explained. "I tried to stop her, but she wouldn't listen. Eventually, I convinced her to sober up a bit before driving home."

Ten shots? Ethan was taken aback by the amount Ava had consumed. "Babe?" He gently shook her, trying to rouse her from her stupor.

Ava slowly opened her eyes, her expression brightening instantly at the sight of Ethan. "Ethan!" she exclaimed with a drunken glee, clumsily opening her arms for a hug. She seemed adorably childlike in her intoxicated state.

As she wrapped her arms around his neck, Ava looked up at him with a mix of happiness and inebriation. "When did you get here?"

"Just now. It's time to head home," Ethan said, helping her to stand. Ava wobbled slightly on her feet.

"You know, I drank a lot of vodka," Ava said with a grin, seemingly proud of her feat. "Like, a whole lot!" She stretched her arms wide to emphasize.

"I can see that," Ethan replied with a soft chuckle, finding her drunken antics somewhat endearing. "But no more vodka for you, young lady," he added playfully.

Ava suddenly stopped, turning to face him with a pout. "What? No! I need it, baby." Her eyes began to well up as she looked into Ethan's face. Gently, she caressed his cheek, her tears now freely flowing. "I'm hurting, babe. Can't you see it?"

Ethan felt a pang in his heart at her tears and the evident pain in her eyes. "Why are you crying?" he asked, his voice laced with worry. He had never seen her so distraught, so visibly broken.

Before she could answer, Ava's lips quivered, and she passed out again, collapsing into Ethan's arms. The weight of her sorrow was palpable, leaving Ethan to carry her, both

THE ILLUSION OF US

physically and emotionally, out of the bar and back into their home.

Ava's head throbbed painfully, each pulse feeling like a hammer against her skull. Trying to sit up, the room spun, and she quickly lay back down, her hand instinctively going to her forehead in an attempt to soothe the pounding ache. "What happened? When did I get back?" she murmured to herself, her last clear memory being her conversation with Brian at the bar.

The bedroom door creaked open, and Ethan appeared, carrying a tray laden with food. His presence was a comforting sight in her disoriented state. "Oh, you're awake. You've been out all day," he said with a warm smile, setting the tray on the bed. "I made you some hangover soup. Bet you're regretting all that vodka now," he added, a playful tease in his tone.

"How did you find out?" Ava asked, her voice still heavy with the remnants of sleep and alcohol.

"I tried calling you when you weren't home. A guy answered your phone and told me where you were. So, I went to pick you up," Ethan explained, taking a seat on the velvet chaise beside the bed.

A soft "Oh..." was all she managed in response, her mind still reeling from the events of the previous night. She began eating the soup, its warmth and flavor a balm to her unsettled stomach.

Ethan's eyes held a deep concern as he observed her. "Is everything okay, babe? You've never gotten that drunk before, and you seemed really upset last night."

Hiding her turmoil behind a smile, she replied, "Just wedding jitters, you know how it is with women." Her attempt at humor felt hollow even to her own ears.

"You sure? You know you can always talk to me about anything, right?" Ethan's voice was gentle, reassuring.

"Of course, babe," she forced another smile, focusing back on the soup. Inside, her heart was a maelstrom of emotions – love, sorrow, and a deep, unspoken fear of the future. As she ate, Ava wrestled with her feelings, knowing that each day brought her closer to a decision that would change both their lives forever.

That evening, Ethan and Ava joined their friends at the airport for a bittersweet farewell to their friend Fred. The group, including Violet, gathered in a close-knit circle. When Fred hugged Ava, it lingered a little longer, a bit more meaningful.

"I'll definitely be there for your wedding, Ava. Wouldn't miss it for the world," he whispered, his voice tinged with emotion.

"Just stay safe, Fred. And remember, we're just a call away if you need anything," Ava reassured him, offering a supportive smile as they parted from their embrace.

As Fred collected his luggage, his flight announcement echoed through the terminal. "Time to head out, guys. Take care, and see you all soon!" The group waved him off, their faces a mix of smiles and sadness.

As they were about to leave, Violet suddenly stopped, her eyes glued to her phone. "Oh no! Ethan!" she exclaimed, causing everyone to halt. "Ethan, I don't know what to do," she said, her voice breaking.

"What's wrong, Vi?" Sofia inquired, concern etched on her face. But Violet, overwhelmed, rushed to Ethan and embraced him. The others exchanged surprised glances.

Ava's heart dropped as Ethan's hand slipped from hers, his attention now fully on comforting Violet. "What happened, Vi?" he asked, concern in his voice.

"My dad's been taken to the hospital. They're at Greenwood Medical Center, Ethan, where you work. I need to get there. Please, can you drive me?" Violet's grip on him tightened, her sobs muffled against his chest.

Amy stepped in, trying to defuse the situation, "Vi, we can drive you there. It's on our way home."

But Violet was insistent, her eyes pleading with Ethan. "No, I need Ethan to take me. Please, Ethan?"

Ethan, caught in the moment, agreed softly, "Of course, I'll take you."

Ava stood frozen as they began to walk away, the realization hitting her that Ethan had forgotten her in the moment. She felt a sting, witnessing Violet's influence over him.

Trying to keep her composure, Ava watched in silence.

"Ethan, what about Ava?" Amy interjected, bringing his attention back to Ava.

Ethan turned, guilt washing over his face. "Babe, I... I'm sorry. I just thought... Violet's dad knows me, and she shouldn't be alone," he stammered, his apology hanging in the air.

Sensing the tension, Tony stepped forward. "Ethan, let me drive Violet. Ava doesn't look well. You should take her home."

Violet, visibly annoyed, clung tighter to Ethan, her actions speaking louder than words.

Ethan looked between Ava and Violet, torn. "Babe, I..."

Violet, impatient, cut in, "Ava, please understand. I really need Ethan right now."

Ava, masking her hurt with a forced smile, replied, "It's fine. Go ahead, Ethan. I'll manage."

As Ethan and Violet turned to leave, Ava grabbed his arm. "Wait, you forgot something," she said, pulling him into a deep, meaningful kiss, an act that visibly irked Violet. Their friends watched, a mix of surprise and admiration.

"Take care of her, Ethan. And give my best to your father, Violet. Hope he recovers soon," Ava said, her voice steady.

"Thanks," Violet replied curtly, her annoyance evident.

As Ethan and Violet walked away, Ava clenched her fists, the pain and turmoil within her almost too much to bear. She stood tall, refusing to let her friends see the depth of her anguish, even though the recent events had made the cracks in her facade all too apparent.

Jasmine drove them to a club that was recommended by her co-worker. As they arrived, Ava recognized it as the same club she had visited the night before. Despite its sophisticated appearance, it was surprisingly uncrowded, just like last night.

They settled into a table in the VIP open area, a secluded spot with a luxurious feel. The club itself was a blend of modern sophistication and cozy comfort. Soft, ambient lighting bathed the room, highlighting the plush velvet seating and sleek, polished bar. Artistic decor pieces added an air of exclusivity, making the space feel both intimate and elegant.

As they looked over the menu, they ordered an assortment of high-end drinks and food. Their selection included artisanal cocktails crafted with premium spirits and fresh, exotic ingredients. For food, they chose gourmet small plates like truffle-infused risotto balls, seared scallops on a bed of microgreens, and a charcuterie board featuring imported cheeses and cured meats.

"This place is so cozy, Jaz," Sofia commented, admiring the club's chic interior.

"I know, right?" Jasmine responded. "It's so private and intimate. My friend Lacy raved about it."

Ava sat quietly, her thoughts consumed with Ethan and Violet. Her friends' chatter was a distant buzz against the backdrop of her inner turmoil.

Amy nudged her gently. "You okay?" she whispered.

Ava managed a sad smile. "Ye...yeah."

Jasmine couldn't help but vent her frustration. "Ava, you should've pulled Vi's hair earlier. She acted like she's Ethan's girlfriend. So annoying."

Sofia tried to offer a different perspective. "Maybe she was really worried because her dad was taken to the hospital. She wouldn't have acted like that otherwise, right Ava?"

Their order arrived, and Ava took a deep sip of her drink, trying to drown her sorrows.

Jasmine countered Sofia's argument. "It doesn't matter. What she did was insensitive, especially in front of Ava."

Sofia gave Ava a worried look, trying to change the subject. "Is everything okay with you and Ethan?"

Ava hesitated before replying, "Everything's fine, girls. We're good," her smile not quite reaching her eyes.

Sofia and Jasmine seemed relieved by her response.

As Ava and her friends enjoyed their evening, their attention was suddenly captured by a man approaching their table. "Look who's back for more," he quipped, his eyes twinkling with humor. "Two nights in a row, huh? I'm starting to think you're a fan of the place, Ava."

Her friends, curious, leaned in. "Do you know him, Ava?" they asked.

Squinting, Ava recognized him. "Brian?" she said, a bit surprised.

Brian grinned lopsidedly, revealing his strikingly handsome features. He had a well-built physique that complemented his attractive face, and his charming smile was infectious.

"Who is he, Ava?" Jasmine couldn't help but ask, clearly taken by his good looks.

"We met yesterday. He's a bartender here," Ava explained, feeling a touch embarrassed.

"You were here last night?" Amy asked, surprised.

Ava nodded. "Yeah, just stumbled upon the place."

Brian chuckled, his laughter warm and inviting. "Stumbled is one way to put it. But hey, I'm not complaining. You're practically an investor now!" He then added, "Actually, I own this joint. We just opened a few days ago. Thanks for giving us a shot, Ava. Tonight, your drinks are on me. Don't hold back on the order!"

The girls were clearly delighted. "That's incredibly sweet of you, Brian. Thank you!" Jasmine exclaimed.

Brian flashed them a playful smile. "Enjoy your night, ladies," he said. His gaze lingered on Ava for a moment longer. "Great seeing you again, Ava," he added, his voice tinged with genuine warmth.

As Brian walked away, Jasmine couldn't contain her excitement. "Ava, Brian is seriously hot! I'd totally date him if I weren't already taken."

Amy joined in, smiling mischievously. "Did you see the way he looked at you, Ava? I think he's got a thing for you."

Jasmine nudged Ava playfully. "Looks like you made quite the impression."

Ava, trying to deflect the attention, laughed it off. "He's just being friendly, guys."

Sofia, joining in the teasing, said, "Seems like Brian's quite smitten with you, Ava. Just don't forget you're soon to be a married woman!"

Their laughter and playful banter provided a much-needed distraction for Ava, though deep down, her heart was still weighed down by the turmoil of her situation with Ethan and Violet.

CHAPTER ELEVEN

Ava woke up to an unsettling quiet in their home, Ethan's side of the bed untouched. Checking her phone, her heart sank - no missed calls, no messages from Ethan. She tried calling him, but it went straight to voicemail, leaving her with a heavy heart and unshed tears.

Fighting the despair, Ava headed for a steamy shower, hoping to wash away not just the physical remnants of yesterday but also the icy coldness enveloping her heart. Throughout the day, she buried herself in work, refusing to dwell on Ethan's absence, yet her mind constantly drifted back to him. Her efforts to reach him went unanswered, his silence amplifying her worries.

As evening approached without any word from Ethan, Ava decided to visit the hospital. On the way, she bought flowers and fruits for Violet's father, a gesture of goodwill amidst her own turmoil.

Upon reaching the hospital, Ava's eyes scanned the hallway and caught a glimpse of Ethan, walking briskly with fellow residents. "Ethan! Babe!" she called, but he was too far away, too engrossed in his phone call, and soon hurried off in the opposite direction. Ava's heart sank further; he was here, alive and well, yet so far away from her.

With a heavy heart, Ava continued to Mr. Stein's room. She hesitated at the door, overhearing a conversation that sent a jolt through her.

"So, are you and Ethan getting back together?" she heard Mr. Stein inquire, a playful tone in his voice.

"Dad, please..." Violet's voice was tinged with embarrassment.

Ethan's voice was missing from the exchange, but Mr. Stein's laughter was clear. "You're making Ethan uncomfortable," Violet chided her father.

Ava steeled herself and entered the room, her presence immediately changing the atmosphere. "Ava..." Ethan's voice was laced with surprise. Violet's reaction was subtle, a quick roll of her eyes betraying her annoyance.

Ignoring the tension, Ava smiled and placed the gifts on the table. "I brought these for you, Mr. Stein. I hope they help you feel better."

Mr. Stein's smile was genuine. "Thank you, young lady. And who might you be?"

Ava met Ethan's and Violet's eyes briefly before answering confidently. "I'm Ethan's fiancée."

The room went silent, Mr. Stein's expression turning to one of shock. "Oh, Ethan, you're getting married?" he asked, sadness creeping into his voice.

Ethan could only muster a weak smile. Ava, pushing past the awkwardness, cheerfully said, "Yes, we are. Our wedding is in just two weeks."

Mr. Stein nodded, his happiness forced. "I see. Well, congratulations."

Soon after, Ethan led Ava out into the corridor, his face a mix of emotions. "Ava, is there something you wanted to talk about?" he asked, finally turning to face her.

Ava's heart was racing. "Why didn't you come home last night, babe? You didn't even call."

Ethan's expression softened, guilt washing over his features. "I'm sorry. I was caught up here. Mr. Stein had a heart attack, and I stayed to help with the tests. I didn't mean to worry you."

Ava nodded, her smile forced. "It's okay. I was just concerned."

Ethan reached for her hands. "I promise, it won't happen again, babe."

Ava quickly wrapped up the conversation, eager to leave. "I should get going. You have work, and I... I have things to do too."

With a quick peck on Ethan's cheek, she left, not waiting for a response, her heart heavier than before. She needed space, space to breathe, space to think away from the hospital, away from the complexities of her relationship with Ethan.

Ava felt a growing distance between her and Ethan, despite his regular return home after Mr. Stein's discharge. They shared the same space, yet the emotional gap was widening each day. She was determined to bridge this gap, to rekindle the closeness they once shared, but Ethan seemed distant, almost unreachable.

Nevertheless, Ava held onto hope, especially when Ethan agreed to accompany her to the wedding venue to finalize the arrangements with their wedding coordinator. She saw this as an opportunity for them to spend some quality time together, something they hadn't done in a while.

At the venue, their coordinator, Marissa, greeted them with enthusiasm. "Ava, Ethan, it's great to see you both! We have quite a bit to cover for your big day!"

As they sat down, Marissa began discussing the details. "Firstly, let's confirm your guest list. We need the final headcount for the caterers."

Ava nodded, enthusiastically engaging in the conversation. "We've managed to narrow it down. I'll send you the updated list by tonight."

"That's perfect," Marissa replied. "Now, let's talk about the setup. We were thinking of having the ceremony outdoors, under the oak trees. The natural light at sunset will be perfect for photos."

Ava's eyes lit up. "That sounds beautiful! I love the idea of an outdoor ceremony at sunset."

Marissa then brought out a tablet to show them some floral arrangement options. "For your centerpieces, we're thinking a mix of roses and lilies. It'll complement the rustic theme you're going for."

Ava leaned in, examining the images closely. "Can we add some peonies to that mix? I've always loved peonies."

"Of course, we can do that," Marissa smiled. "Now, regarding the reception, we've planned a three-course meal. For starters, how do you feel about a seasonal salad, followed by a choice of salmon or filet mignon, and a decadent chocolate mousse for dessert?"

"That sounds delicious," Ava replied, trying to catch Ethan's eye for his opinion.

Ethan, however, seemed distant. His responses were noncommittal, his gaze often drifting away from the conversation. "Yeah, sounds good," he muttered, barely glancing at the tablet.

Marissa, sensing the tension, tried to engage Ethan. "Ethan, what are your thoughts on the music selection for the reception? Any particular band or DJ you'd like?"

Ethan gave a half-hearted shrug. "Whatever Ava thinks is best," he said, his attention seemingly elsewhere.

Ava felt a pang of disappointment. She had hoped this meeting would bring them closer, reignite some spark, but Ethan's detachment was palpable. The excitement she felt about the wedding details was tempered by his lack of interest, casting a shadow over what should have been a joyous preparation for their future together.

As the meeting concluded, Ava thanked Marissa and they left the venue.

The drive home felt longer than usual, each mile adding to Ava's apprehension. As they pulled into their driveway, the reality of their situation settled in. They were just weeks away from their wedding, yet the distance between them felt insurmountable. Ava knew she needed to confront these fears, to understand where Ethan stood, but the fear of his potential answer left her paralyzed, caught between the love she still felt and the painful possibility that she might be losing him.

As they arrived home, Ethan noticed Ava's subdued demeanor. "Are you feeling sick, babe?" he asked, concern flickering in his eyes. He reached out to check her forehead, but Ava subtly dodged his touch.

She offered a weak smile. "Maybe I'm just tired. I think a bath will help me feel better."

Ethan nodded understandingly. "Alright. I'll make something for us to eat," he suggested, ready to head to the kitchen.

Ava, wanting to break the growing tension between them, took a chance to lighten the mood. "Do you want to join me in the bath instead?" she asked playfully, hoping to rekindle some of their lost intimacy.

Ethan seemed momentarily taken aback by her invitation, then a playful smirk crossed his face. "Hmm, tempting..." he responded, yet Ava could sense his hesitation, the playful tone not quite reaching his eyes.

"I'll go ahead then. See you in a bit, babe," Ava said quickly, turning towards the bathroom. Once inside, she turned on the faucet, letting the tub fill with warm water. Alone and hidden by the steam and the sound of running water, she finally allowed her tears to flow freely.

The hot tears mixed with the warm water, each one a silent testament to the confusion and pain she felt. Ava's attempt at closeness had fallen flat, leaving her more isolated than before. As she sank into the bath, her thoughts were a tumultuous mix of fear, sadness, and longing for the connection they once shared. The uncertainty of their future, once a distant thought, was now a looming presence, overshadowing even the most mundane moments of their daily life.

Ava's heart ached with the weight of unspoken words and unresolved feelings. She wasn't ready to let him go, but the fear that he wanted to leave was like a constant shadow, darkening even her brightest thoughts.

The water, once warm, began to cool, mirroring the cold dread settling in her heart. How long could she hold onto a love that felt like it was slowly, inexorably fading? How could she fight for someone who seemed already half gone? These questions haunted her, unanswered, as she lay there, alone with her thoughts, in the fading warmth of her bath.

The night before their trip to Colorado, Ava and Ethan prepared for an early night. Ethan was engrossed in reading some medical papers on the bed when Ava joined him. Sensing an opportunity for closeness, she moved nearer and began massaging his shoulders, relieved to hear him groan with satisfaction.

"You've been so caught up with work lately, baby. Your shoulders are so tense," she commented, her fingers working gently on his muscles. "You should take a moment to relax," she added, her voice taking on a sultry tone, signaling her deeper desire.

Ava missed their intimacy. She caressed his arms seductively, trying to set a romantic mood. Ethan chuckled softly as her kisses landed on his shoulders. "Babe, what are you trying to do?" he asked, amused yet distracted.

"I really need to study these papers, babe. Dr. Randolph is letting me scrub in on a cardiopulmonary bypass surgery next week. I want to be fully prepared," he explained, but his chuckle betrayed his enjoyment of her affection.

"It can wait," Ava whispered seductively in his ear, eliciting another groan from him. She smiled secretly, sensing her effect on him. "We haven't been this intimate in weeks, Ethan. I miss you. I want you," she confessed softly.

Ethan tried to maintain his composure, gently resisting her advances. "Babe, I—"

"Don't you want me?" she asked, her voice tinged with hurt and disappointment.

"That's not it," Ethan replied, his hand caressing her cheek tenderly.

"Then let's not wait," Ava insisted, her smile playful yet filled with longing. Just as she leaned in for a kiss, Ethan's phone rang. He quickly jumped off the bed to answer it.

"Babe, let me just take this call. It's Dr. Randolph, could be important. I'll be right back," he said, winking playfully as he stepped out onto the balcony.

Ava nodded, forcing a smile, but as Ethan stepped away, her heart sank. She caught a glimpse of the caller ID; it wasn't Dr. Randolph. It was Violet.

Alone in the room, Ava fought back tears. She lay down, closing her eyes, the weight of her sadness too much to bear. She didn't wait for Ethan to return; sleep was her only escape now.

When Ethan returned, Ava was already asleep. He sat beside her, staring at her peaceful face. A wave of guilt washed over him. The realization of how distant he had become since Violet's return hit him hard. He thought of the pain it would cause Ava if he left her.

Ava had always been loving and supportive, undeserving of any hurt, especially not from him. Ethan sighed heavily, his hand gently caressing her face. The idea of hurting her was unbearable, yet the pressure from Violet and his own conflicting feelings left him torn.

In the quiet of the room, with Ava sleeping beside him, Ethan whispered a sorrowful apology. "I'm sorry..." His voice was laden with regret and sadness, a silent confession to the sleeping figure beside him. The complexity of his emotions -

guilt, confusion, and a deep-seated sense of loyalty - left him torn between his past with Violet and the present, potentially fading, with Ava.

CHAPTER TWELVE

At the luxurious cabin in Breckenridge, Colorado, Ava and Ethan gathered with their close friends for a weekend ski trip. The cabin, nestled amidst snowy slopes, offered a stunning view of the wintry landscape. Their group included Tony, Carlson, Amy, Sofia, Jasmine, Troy, Joan, Brent, and, notably, Violet.

As they settled in, the cabin buzzed with excitement.

"So, who's ready to hit the slopes this afternoon?" Tony asked, grinning widely as he looked around at the group.

"Count me in!" Jasmine exclaimed, her enthusiasm infectious. "I've been waiting for this trip for weeks."

Carlson, pulling on his ski gloves, nodded in agreement. "Same here. The snow conditions are perfect today."

Ava, trying to keep the mood light, chimed in. "I bet Ethan's going to show off his skiing skills again. Remember last time?"

Ethan, who had been somewhat quiet, smiled. "I don't know about showing off, but I'm definitely looking forward to some good runs."

Violet, standing a bit apart from the group, added, "Ethan's always been a great skier. I'm sure he'll be leading the pack."

There was a brief, awkward silence before Amy quickly changed the subject. "So, who's up for some hot chocolate when we get back? I heard the cabin's stocked with all the goodies."

Sofia clapped her hands excitedly. "Oh, I'm all for that! And maybe some board games by the fireplace?"

Brent, who was checking his ski equipment, looked up. "Board games sound great. And I'm totally winning at Monopoly this time."

Joan laughed. "In your dreams, Brent! I'm the reigning Monopoly champion here."

Troy joined in the banter. "We'll see about that. I've been practicing my strategic skills."

As they continued to chat and joke, Ava noticed Ethan frequently glancing at his phone, his attention divided. Despite the lively atmosphere, a sense of unease lingered around him.

After a while, the group geared up and headed out to the ski slopes. The crisp mountain air and the thrill of skiing brought a temporary respite from the undercurrents of tension.

On the snowy slopes of Breckenridge, the group was in high spirits, energized by the thrill of skiing. Ethan, with his usual skill and confidence, was effortlessly navigating the slopes, but it wasn't his prowess that caught Ava's attention. Throughout the afternoon, Ethan had been devoting a significant amount of his time to Violet, patiently teaching her how to ski.

Ava watched from a distance, a pang of sadness in her heart as she observed Ethan's attentiveness towards Violet. He was gentle and patient, guiding her through the basics, his laughter echoing every time Violet managed to stay upright. To the casual observer, they appeared close, almost intimate in their interactions.

"Ethan really seems to be enjoying teaching Violet," Tony commented, noticing Ava's gaze.

"Yeah, he's always been a great teacher," Ava replied, her voice tinged with a melancholy she couldn't quite hide.

Sofia, skiing up beside Ava, offered a sympathetic smile. "It's sweet of him to help her out. It's her first time skiing, right?"

Ava nodded, forcing a smile. "Yeah, she's lucky to have such a patient instructor."

As the group continued skiing, Ava tried to focus on her own enjoyment of the sport, but her mind was elsewhere, troubled by the easy camaraderie she saw between Ethan and Violet. The laughter and shouts of their friends faded into the background as Ava's thoughts lingered on the growing distance in her relationship with Ethan.

The afternoon wore on, the sun beginning to dip behind the mountains, casting long shadows on the snow. The group decided to head back to the cabin, their spirits high from the day's adventures. Ava trailed behind, her mind heavy with unspoken concerns.

Back at the cabin, as everyone settled into the comfort of the warm interior, Ava saw an opportunity to spend some alone time with Ethan. She approached him, hoping to rekindle their connection.

"Ethan, do you want to go for a walk? Just the two of us?" Ava suggested, her voice hopeful.

Ethan, about to respond, was interrupted by Violet. "Ethan, could you help me with my ski boots? They're really stuck," Violet called out from across the room, her tone suggesting more than a simple request for assistance.

Ethan, caught in a moment of hesitation, finally nodded at Ava. "Sure, a walk sounds nice. Give me just a second to help Vi."

Ava watched as Ethan went over to help Violet, her heart sinking a little more with each passing moment. The brief interaction between them seemed unnecessarily prolonged, with Violet laughing softly at something Ethan said.

After a few minutes, Ethan returned to Ava. "Okay, let's go for that walk," he said, though Ava could sense his distraction.

As they stepped outside, the crisp mountain air felt refreshing. Ava tried to initiate conversation. "The scenery here is breathtaking, isn't it?"

THE ILLUSION OF US

"It is," Ethan agreed, but his attention was short-lived. His phone buzzed, and he glanced at the screen. It was Violet again, this time asking if he had seen her gloves.

Ethan sighed. "I need to check on this, babe. Vi's asking about her gloves. Be right back," he said, already heading back to the cabin.

Ava stood there, a mix of frustration and sadness washing over her. She waited for Ethan, but when he returned, it was with news of another request from Violet.

"Vi's feeling a bit cold. She's asking if I could make her some hot tea. You know how she's always been sensitive to the cold," Ethan explained, almost apologetically.

Ava tried to mask her disappointment. "Sure, go ahead. I'll wait here."

Inside, as Ethan attended to Violet, Ava's friends noticed the dynamic. Tony leaned in to Ava, "Is everything okay, Ava? You seem a bit off."

Ava forced a smile. "Just tired, I guess."

As the evening progressed, Ava's attempts to connect with Ethan were continually interrupted by Violet's calls for his attention. With each interruption, Ava felt more like an outsider, watching as the bond she once shared with Ethan seemed to slip further away.

Feeling overwhelmed by the continuous interactions between Ethan and Violet, Ava needed a moment to herself. She quietly slipped out to the patio, seeking solace in the serene wintry

THE ILLUSION OF US

landscape outside. The patio, blanketed in soft white snow and surrounded by towering pines, offered a peaceful retreat from the cabin's bustling atmosphere.

Standing there, Ava wrapped her hands around a warm cup of hot cocoa, the steam gently rising into the cold air. The quiet beauty of the snow-covered surroundings brought a sense of calm, momentarily easing the sadness in her heart. Ava had always loved winter, the way the snow seemed to cover the world in a blanket of purity and quiet.

As she sipped her cocoa, the tranquility of the scene allowed her to reflect. The snowflakes gently falling from the sky reminded her of the fleeting nature of moments and feelings. She thought about her relationship with Ethan, how it used to be warm and comforting like her drink, but now felt as cold as the air around her.

Lost in thought, Ava barely noticed the soft crunch of footsteps approaching. It was Amy, likely coming to check on her. But in that moment, Ava didn't mind the company. The peacefulness of the patio, coupled with the beauty of the night, had given her a much-needed respite, a moment of clarity amidst the complexities of her emotions.

Amy, sensing Ava's distress, joined her on the patio, her expression one of concern. She couldn't help but notice how Ethan's attention had been monopolized by Violet throughout the day. "Aren't you going to call your fiancé, Ava? He's been with Vi all day. You should call him in here," she suggested, her annoyance at the situation evident in her voice.

Ava, gazing out at the snow-covered landscape, managed a weak smile. "I'm tired, Ames. I'm so tired of fighting for my fiancé's attention. I'm just... really exhausted," she murmured, her voice barely above a whisper as she let out a heavy sigh.

Amy looked at Ava, her heart aching at the sight of her friend's weariness. Ava's usual vibrance seemed dimmed, her eyes reflecting a deep exhaustion that went beyond physical tiredness. It was as if the constant struggle to hold onto Ethan, to maintain the facade of a happy relationship in the face of Violet's presence, was draining her.

Choosing not to press the issue further, Amy simply sat beside Ava in supportive silence. The quiet companionship offered a small comfort, a recognition of the unspoken pain Ava was enduring. In that moment, Amy realized that Ava was nearing her breaking point, on the verge of giving up on the fight for a relationship that seemed increasingly one-sided.

The two friends sat together, sharing the quiet of the snowy evening, each lost in their own thoughts. For Ava, the serenity of the setting was a stark contrast to the turmoil within her, a reminder of the peace she longed for in her own life.

Ava slipped quietly into their room, where Ethan was deeply engrossed in his research materials for the upcoming cardiopulmonary bypass surgery. His attention shifted as he noticed her entrance. "Where've you been, babe? I was looking for you earlier," he inquired, a hint of concern in his voice.

Ava managed a weak smile, the fatigue evident in her eyes. "I was just outside... talking to Amy," she replied, her voice low. Without further conversation, she made her way to the bathroom for a warm bath, seeking solace in the soothing water.

After her bath, Ava returned to the bedroom, slipping silently under the covers next to Ethan. She lay there, enveloped in the warmth of the blanket, but her silence was heavy with unspoken thoughts.

Ethan, sensing something wasn't right, turned his attention to her. "You okay, babe?" he asked, his voice laced with concern.

"Yeah..." Ava's response was brief, lacking its usual warmth.

Ethan moved closer, his medical instinct kicking in. "Are you sick, babe?" he asked gently, reaching out to touch her forehead. "You're quite warm," he noted with worry. He quickly rummaged through his bag and retrieved a bottle of fever medicine. "Here, take this before you sleep," he suggested, handing her the medicine.

Ava wordlessly took the medicine, her thoughts drifting. Perhaps, she mused, it could alleviate the ache in her heart as well. "Thanks. Good night," she murmured, her voice barely above a whisper.

"Good night, babe. Rest well," Ethan replied, leaning in to kiss her forehead. The tenderness of his gesture was a stark reminder of the affection that once flowed freely between them. It almost broke Ava's resolve, the sweetness of the moment contrasting sharply with the emotional distance that had grown between them.

As Ethan returned to his reading, Ava lay there in the dark, the weight of her emotions pressing down on her. The kiss on her forehead, once a simple act of affection, now felt like a rare oasis in the desert of their strained relationship.

The next day, the group decided to take it easy at the cabin, conserving their energy for the evening's festivities – Ethan and Ava's Jack and Jill party. Ava, despite feeling slightly under the weather, put on a brave face, determined not to dampen the celebratory spirit her friends had worked hard to create.

As the evening approached, their friends whisked Ethan and Ava away to separate parts of the cabin for a surprise transformation. Ava was dressed in a stunning cocktail dress that accentuated her features elegantly. The dress, a deep shade of midnight blue, complemented her eyes and was paired with tasteful, sparkling accessories. Her hair was styled in soft waves that framed her face, highlighting her natural beauty and grace. Despite her earlier fatigue, Ava radiated a serene and sophisticated charm.

Ethan, on the other hand, looked dapper in a tailored suit that fit him perfectly. The dark suit, paired with a crisp white shirt and a sleek tie, brought out his handsome features. His hair was styled neatly, adding to his sharp and suave appearance. Together, they looked like the epitome of an elegant and loving couple.

The party's decorations were a beautiful blend of both their tastes. The cabin was transformed into a cozy yet chic party space, with fairy lights strung across the ceiling, casting a soft, warm glow over the room. Elegant floral arrangements adorned the tables, and a banner with "Ethan & Ava's Jack and Jill Party" hung prominently. The ambiance was both romantic and festive, with a touch of rustic charm that complemented the cabin's natural setting.

As Ethan and Ava were led back into the main party area, their friends greeted them with cheers and applause. The couple was genuinely surprised and touched by the effort put into the decorations.

The atmosphere inside the cabin was electric, the room alive with laughter and the clinking of glasses as Ethan and Ava were ushered in by their jubilant friends.

"Look at these two lovebirds!" Tony exclaimed, raising his glass. "To Ethan and Ava, the soon-to-be newlyweds!"

Sofia approached, her eyes shining with happiness. "You both look absolutely gorgeous! This party is going to be legendary!"

Ethan, scanning the beautifully decorated room, replied with a modest smile, "This is amazing, guys. Thanks for going all out."

Ava, her eyes sparkling despite her earlier weariness, added, "I can't thank you all enough. This means the world to us."

The evening kicked off with lively games. Amy announced the first one, "Time for 'How Well Do You Know Your Partner?' Ethan, Ava, you're up first!"

The couple shared laughs and playful banter as they answered questions, their friends cheering them on. Despite Ethan's slightly reserved demeanor, he participated, though his enthusiasm was somewhat subdued compared to Ava's.

As the party progressed, Violet's discomfort became increasingly evident. She struggled to mask her displeasure, especially as Ethan and Ava stood hand in hand, sharing light-hearted moments with their friends.

The mood escalated when Brent, acting as the DJ, announced, "It's dance-off time! Let's see which couple has the best moves!"

The floor erupted with cheers as couples, including Ethan and Ava, showed off their dance moves. Ava, immersed in the fun, briefly forgot her worries, laughing and swaying to the music. Ethan, while not as exuberant, kept up, his movements more restrained.

In the midst of the laughter and dancing, Violet quietly slipped out, her exit barely noticed amidst the revelry. Her departure went largely unremarked, except by a few who saw the unhappy expression she couldn't quite hide.

Amidst the lively chatter and laughter with her friends, Ava suddenly realized that Ethan was no longer in the room. Excusing herself, she began to search for him, a sense of unease growing within her. She checked their room, then the living room, and even the patio, but he was nowhere to be found. With a growing sense of apprehension, Ava stepped outside, moving to the quieter side of the cabin.

There, under the dim glow of the exterior lights, she found Ethan, in a scene that felt like a nightmare unfolding before her eyes. Violet was crying, her body leaning against Ethan's chest.

"Ethan, when are you going to tell her about us? We can't keep hiding like this," Violet implored, her voice heavy with emotion. "Are you really going to go through with the wedding?"

Ethan, his face etched with conflict, attempted to quiet her. "Vi, please, keep it down."

But Violet's desperation only intensified. "How can you stand there with Ava, pretending everything is fine, when you know how I feel? Do you even love her?"

There was a tense pause, the weight of her question hanging in the air.

Violet pressed further, her voice breaking. "Ethan, please, just tell me... do you love her?"

Ethan's response came in a hesitant whisper, barely audible. "No... I love you." But his hesitation was lost in the moment, unnoticed by Violet.

At that instant, Violet closed the distance between them with a kiss.

Ava, hidden in the shadows, involuntarily let out a gasp, her presence suddenly revealed. As Ethan and Violet turned to face her, Ethan looked like a man torn apart, a mix of guilt and confusion in his eyes, while Violet appeared unapologetically triumphant.

Frozen in place, Ava's heart shattered in silence. The scene unfolding before her confirmed her deepest fears, turning them into a harsh reality. The night, meant to be a celebration of their union, had instead become a poignant display of its unraveling.

CHAPTER THIRTEEN

Ava ran blindly, her mind a whirlwind of pain and betrayal. The cold air stung her cheeks, but it was nothing compared to the ache in her heart. She had known deep down that Ethan might leave her for Violet, but witnessing it, especially on a night that was supposed to be theirs, was a pain beyond anything she could have imagined.

Her vision blurred by tears, Ava ran, each step fueled by a tumult of emotions she couldn't contain. Betrayal, hurt, shock – they all merged into a crushing wave of despair.

As she finally slowed, her breaths came in shuddering sobs. She found herself at a secluded spot, away from the lights and sounds of the cabin. Here, under the indifferent canopy of the night sky, she allowed herself to fully feel the extent of her heartache. She was not just crying over Ethan's betrayal, but also for herself, for the time and love she had invested in a relationship that was now ending in the most painful way imaginable.

Her body shook with sobs, each one a release of the pain, disappointment, and love that she had held onto for so long. She knew this was more than just the end of her relationship with Ethan; it was the closing of a significant chapter of her life. The coldness of the night enveloped her, yet it was nothing compared to the numbness spreading through her heart, a defense against a pain too overwhelming to fully comprehend.

Ava's steps were resolute as she approached the cabin, her mind still reeling, but determined to maintain her composure. Violet, waiting at the gate, seemed intent on confronting her. Ava tried to pass by without engaging, but Violet reached out and grabbed her arm.

"Now that you know about Ethan and me, you should be the one to call off the engagement," Violet stated coldly, without a hint of remorse.

Ava took a deep breath, steadying her emotions before responding with a sharp gaze. "Get your hand off me, Vi. I don't have the time or energy for this." Her voice was firm, dismissive. "And why should I be the one to break off the engagement?"

Violet, undeterred, met her gaze with a hard look. "You saw us kiss. Ethan loves me, not you," she declared with a sense of entitlement.

Ava let out a derisive laugh, her patience wearing thin. "Really, Vi? I never knew you could be so shameless. To think you'd try to steal a friend's fiancé."

"He was mine first. I love him!" Violet shot back defiantly.

Ava's smirk was bitter. "And then you left him. That's some 'love' you have there." She paused, gathering her strength. "I don't want to hear anymore, Vi. Ethan and I are getting married next week, and that's that. Deal with it."

Leaving Violet standing there, Ava turned and walked away, her head held high. She refused to let Violet see any hint of defeat in her eyes.

As Ava stepped back into the room, she was a picture of composed strength, but upon seeing Ethan, her façade of resilience crumbled. The sight of him, so pensive and troubled, was like a key unlocking the floodgates of her pent-up emotions. The tears she had been holding back cascaded down her cheeks, each one a silent testament to her shattered heart.

Ethan, seeing her in such distress, was filled with guilt and remorse. He rushed to her, enveloping her in his arms in a futile attempt to offer comfort. But his embrace only served as a poignant reminder of what they were about to lose, intensifying her sobs.

"Hush now, baby," Ethan whispered soothingly, his embrace tightening. The tenderness in his voice contrasted sharply with the pain they were both feeling. "I'm so sorry... I never meant for any of this to happen. Please believe me."

Ava, nestled in his arms, couldn't bring herself to be angry. She knew she should have been, but her love for Ethan, a love that had been the cornerstone of her life for six years, overshadowed the bitterness and betrayal. She raised her tear-streaked face to meet his gaze, her eyes a mirror of her broken soul.

In the dimly lit room, Ava's sobbing filled the silence, each tear a wordless expression of the heartache she had endured.

Her voice, when she spoke, was fragile yet laced with the strength of her unwavering love for Ethan.

"All my life, Ethan..." she sobbed, her voice a delicate whisper, trembling with emotion. "I loved you with everything I had. I believed in us, in our love. But when I heard you tell Tony that you never loved me, it was like my world collapsed around me. I was living, but it felt like a part of me had died."

Ava's hand, trembling, reached up to caress his face, her touch a testament to a love that had endured even in the darkest moments. "I tried to be strong, Ethan. For us. I thought if I just loved you enough, we could overcome anything. But every time you looked at Violet, every time you left my side to be with her... it was like a knife twisting in my heart."

Her voice broke as she continued, the words pouring out of her like a dam breaking. "You and Violet... there's something between you that I can't compete with. It's clear to everyone. And I... I can't stand in the way of that."

A heavy silence filled the room, punctuated only by Ava's soft cries. Ethan, tears streaming down his face, was a portrait of regret and loss. He tried to speak, but words failed him.

Ava smiled through her tears, a bittersweet, heart-wrenching smile. "Don't cry, Ethan. I'm saying goodbye because I love you. I can't hold onto you at the cost of your happiness. You deserve to be with someone who you truly love, and if that's not me, then... then I have to let you go."

Her words hung in the air, a final surrender of their love. In that moment, Ava's heartbreak was palpable, a raw, exposed wound for which there was no immediate healing.

In that moment, driven by a maelstrom of emotion – love, regret, longing – Ethan leaned in and kissed Ava. It was a kiss full of everything they had shared and everything they were about to lose. Ava responded, pouring all her love, her pain, her goodbye into that kiss.

Their embrace led them to the bed, their union a poignant and painful farewell. As they made love, Ava's tears never ceased, each one a silent goodbye to the man she had loved with all her heart. In the aftermath, as they lay there in silence, the reality of their parting loomed large, a painful ending to a love story that had once held so much promise.

Ethan jolted awake to the persistent knocking at the door, the remnants of sleep quickly fading as he reached instinctively for Ava beside him. The other side of the bed was empty, the sheets cool and untouched since she had left. Confusion and a sense of foreboding washed over him as he sat up, glancing around the room in a daze. Ava was nowhere to be seen.

"Ethan? Are you awake?" Violet's voice carried through the door, her knocks growing more insistent.

"Ethan, what's going on?" Violet asked as he opened the door, her face brightening with a forced smile.

Brushing past her without a word, Ethan quickly began searching the cabin for Ava. He checked the living room, the kitchen, even the patio where they had spent some quiet moments together, but she wasn't there.

Ethan approached his friends in the living room, his voice laced with urgency. "Have any of you seen Ava this morning?"

Tony, cradling a mug of hot cocoa, looked up in surprise. "Isn't she still in bed? We haven't seen her since you two left the party last night."

Jasmine chimed in, half-joking, "Yeah, you guys were the party poopers of the night."

Frustration and worry creased Ethan's brow as he ran a hand through his hair. The uneasy feeling in his gut was growing stronger. He dashed back to their room to grab his phone, his friends' confused and concerned gazes following him.

"Ethan, is everything alright?" Carlson asked, trailing behind him with Amy.

Amy, just coming out of another room, stopped short at the sight of Ethan's distress. "She's gone," she said softly, capturing everyone's attention. "Ava left last night, around midnight. She wouldn't say why, just that... you two had broken up."

The room fell silent, the weight of her words hanging in the air.

"Is that true, Ethan?" Tony asked, his voice heavy with concern. "Why?" His gaze shifted to Violet, who merely shrugged, a look of indifference on her face.

Ethan leaned against the wall, closing his eyes as the reality of the situation hit him. "I have to go," he muttered, his voice barely audible, and quickly returned to the room to pack his bags.

THE ILLUSION OF US

Violet, following him, asked in a panic, "Ethan, what are you doing?"

"I need to find Ava. I have to... to apologize, to explain," he said, his voice fraught with emotion as he dialed for a cab.

"Ethan, think about us," Violet implored, her voice laced with desperation as she tried to hold him back.

Ethan turned to her, his expression one of frustration and regret. "Vi, this isn't just about us. I can't ignore the hurt I've caused Ava. I need to find her, talk to her, try to make things right in whatever way I can."

Violet's expression shifted to one of disbelief. "But Ethan, she left you. She let you go. Why can't you see that this is our chance to start over?"

He shook his head, his decision firm. "It's not that simple, Vi. I can't just walk away from the hurt I've caused. I owe Ava an explanation, a proper goodbye. This isn't just about what I want anymore."

With those final words, Ethan pulled away from Violet and hurried out of the room, leaving her standing alone, her plans unraveling before her eyes.

His friends, still gathered in the living room, watched him rush past, a mix of concern and confusion on their faces. Ethan's guilt and worry were palpable, his normally calm demeanor replaced by a sense of urgency.

As he left the cabin in search of Ava, the cold morning air hit him, a stark reminder of the reality he now faced. The weight of his actions, the complexity of his feelings for both Ava and Violet, and the uncertainty of what lay ahead consumed him. The drive to find Ava, to offer some semblance of closure, propelled him forward, even as he grappled with the enormity of the emotional turmoil he had caused.

The stark emptiness of the apartment echoed Ethan's feelings as he stepped inside. The darkness enveloped him, mirroring the hollow void that had formed in his heart. He moved through the rooms, each step heavy with the realization that Ava was truly gone. Her clothes, her personal belongings, the little things that made their apartment a home – all were absent, leaving behind a tangible emptiness.

In a daze, Ethan reached for his phone, dialing Ava's number with a trembling hand, but the cold, impersonal tone informed him that her phone was out of coverage. His heart, already heavy with guilt and regret, now raced with worry. Where could she be? Was she safe?

Collapsing to the floor, the weight of his actions crushing him, he whispered to himself, "What have I done?" The words were a painful acknowledgment of the reality he had created. In his pursuit of what he thought he wanted, he had not only hurt Ava but also torn apart the fabric of his own life.

Sitting there in the dark, the silence of the apartment was overwhelming. Ethan had never expected to feel so profoundly alone, so utterly helpless. The end of their relationship, which he had thought was what he wanted, now felt like a gaping wound in his existence.

The realization that he had been the architect of his own sorrow was a bitter pill to swallow. He had envisioned freedom, a new beginning with Violet, but now, in the quiet aftermath of his choices, he found himself grappling with a sense of loss he couldn't have anticipated. The absence of Ava, the woman he had spent years with, who had loved him unconditionally, was more than just a physical void; it was an emotional chasm that seemed impossible to bridge.

As the night stretched on, Ethan remained on the floor, lost in his thoughts, confronting the reality of a future without Ava – a future he had chosen but now seemed so bleak and uncertain. The weight of his decisions, the consequences of his actions, lay heavy on his heart, a reminder of the love he had lost and the pain he had caused.

Early in the morning, with the world still shrouded in the soft hues of dawn, Ethan found himself at the doorstep of the Greenwood residence. His heart, a tumultuous mix of hope and dread, led him there with the faint hope of speaking to Ava. However, upon his arrival, he was met with a somber scene. Ava's parents and her brother Nate were gathered in the living room, a cloud of worry hanging over them.

"She...she left?" Ethan's voice cracked, the words tasting of denial and regret. James Greenwood, Ava's father, fixed a piercing gaze on him.

Mrs. Greenwood's voice, usually so composed, trembled with barely contained emotion. "What's going on, Ethan? Why did Ava leave so abruptly, and just a week before the wedding? She left and said that she wasn't ready to get married and asked for our understanding but said nothing more."

Ethan, feeling a thousand accusing eyes upon him even in the company of three, lowered his gaze in shame. "It's all on me," he confessed, his voice a mere whisper, laden with the weight of his guilt. "Ava saw me... with Violet."

Nate's voice, sharp with disbelief, cut through the tension. "What did Ava see, Ethan? What did you do?"

Mr. Greenwood's patience reached its limit, his voice booming with an authority that demanded immediate answers. "Ethan, I want the full story, and I want it now. My daughter was inconsolable, and I need to know why."

At that moment, Ethan dropped to his knees before Mr. Greenwood, his posture a desperate admission of guilt. "Violet and I, we... Ava saw us kissed," he confessed, his voice choked with remorse.

Nate's suspicion was evident. "Ethan, my sister wouldn't just walk away over a kiss. What are you not telling us?" he demanded, his demeanor tense, ready to confront.

With a heavy heart, Ethan braced himself for the full impact of his truth. "It wasn't just that moment Ava saw. She overheard a conversation between me and Tony... I said things that I can't take back. She overheard my conversation with Tony and had said that I hadn't loved her all those years, and I confessed that I was still in love with my Violet," Ethan confessed, each word laden with shame.

The revelation struck like a thunderbolt, sending shockwaves through the room. Before Ethan could react, Mr. Greenwood's fist connected with his face, flooring him, his lip split, the taste of blood mixing with his regret. "To betray my daughter like this, Ethan?!" Mr. Greenwood roared, his voice shaking with fury and heartache.

Nate sprang into action, grappling with his father. "Dad, stop, this isn't the way!"

James Greenwood's grip on Ethan's collar was relentless, his voice quivering with sorrow and rage. "You shattered the heart of the girl who loved you more than anything. How could you, Ethan?"

Nate, still holding his father back, looked at Ethan, his own anger palpable. "Why bring her hopes up, Ethan? Why propose if your heart wasn't in it?"

Amidst his tears, the pain in Ethan's voice was palpable as he struggled to articulate his remorse. "I don't know. I'm sorry... I thought it was the right thing at the time... I never intended to hurt Ava," he said, his voice breaking under the burden of his guilt. The pain in his eyes was evident, reflecting a deep-seated realization of the hurt he had inflicted. "Seeing the hurt I caused her in her eyes the other night... it changed everything. I'm sorry... All I want now is to take it all back, to fix my mistake."

Finally, Mr. Greenwood's grip loosened, but his voice remained firm and foreboding. "Leave now, Ethan. Before I forget you're my friend's son."

Ethan, visibly shaken and bruised, both physically and emotionally, turned to Mrs. Greenwood. His voice was laden with desperation. "Please, do you know where Ava is? I need to apologize, to make this right."

Tears continued to stream down Mrs. Greenwood's face as she shook her head in response. "We don't know, Ethan. She's gone."

With a final apology, Ethan exited the Greenwood residence. Each step away was heavy with the weight of his remorse, the path to forgiveness and redemption seeming longer and more uncertain than ever before.

CHAPTER FOURTEEN

For the past week, Ethan had been in a state of despair, desperately trying to reach Ava. He had called her family, but they were still as much in the dark as he was. Ethan, unable to process the enormity of his loss, had locked himself in their bedroom, a prisoner of his own regrets. The days blurred into one long, agonizing stretch of solitude, punctuated only by his attempts to contact Ava and the crushing silence that followed.

On what was supposed to be their wedding day, Ethan found himself alone, surrounded by the ghosts of what might have been. The cancellation of the wedding did nothing to alleviate the ache in his heart. Throughout the day, he found himself lost in memories of their time together, the joy they had shared, and the countless ways Ava had shown her love for him. Tears would often escape his eyes as he realized the depth of what he had lost.

He had started dating Ava to spite Violet, to make her jealous, as Violet had always been envious of Ava's privileged life. His initial intention had been to lure Violet back, but she never returned. As time passed, his plan to leave Ava became more complicated.

As Ethan sat alone, lost in his thoughts, he reflected on the path his relationship with Ava had taken. Initially, he had continued the relationship with Ava out of convenience, never finding the right moment to end things without causing pain. He was conscious of not wanting to hurt her, and the fact that his family had grown incredibly fond of her only complicated matters.

Over the years, their lives became increasingly intertwined. Moving in together had seemed like a natural progression, and when he proposed to Ava after six years, it was partly because he recognized how good she was to him, and how deeply she loved him. Violet had been out of his life for so long, and he thought marrying Ava was the right thing to do, especially when his mother entrusted him with the engagement ring his father had given her.

But now, amidst the silence and solitude, Ethan was forced to confront a truth he had long ignored. The happiness he had shared with Ava wasn't just a pretense; it wasn't just going through the motions. Somewhere along the way, without him even realizing it, he had fallen in love with her genuinely and deeply. The care, the laughter, the shared moments – they weren't just acts of going along with the flow; they were real, filled with emotions he hadn't fully understood at the time.

The painful irony was that this realization came too late. Ava had left, and with her departure, the truth of his feelings stood starkly before him. The life they had built, the memories they shared, and the love that had grown in his heart – all were now tinged with regret. Ethan grappled with the harsh reality that he had lost the woman he truly loved, not through a twist of fate, but through his own blindness to his heart's truth.

His heart leaped as he heard the pincode of their door lock beeping. "Ava!" he exclaimed, a surge of hope coursing through him as he rushed to the door.

But that hope shattered as he saw who stood in the doorway. It wasn't Ava, but Nate, her older brother. Ethan's face fell, the brief flicker of hope extinguished, leaving him to face the reality of his loss.

Nate's expression was one of concern as he stepped inside. "Ethan, we need to talk," he said, his voice heavy with unspoken emotions.

Ethan could only nod, the weight of his actions and the magnitude of his loss pressing down on him. The door closed behind Nate, sealing Ethan in with the consequences of his choices, far removed from the future he had once envisioned with Ava.

Nate observed Ethan closely, the worry evident in his eyes. Ethan looked like a shadow of the man he used to be, unkempt and clearly struggling with the weight of his actions. As Ethan set the coffee cups down, the silence that enveloped them was thick with unspoken words.

"Ethan," Nate finally broke the silence, his tone tinged with a mix of humor and concern. "Look at yourself. You haven't shaved in days. You're starting to look like a caveman."

But Ethan barely reacted to the joke, his gaze distant and filled with pain. "Have you heard from Ava?" he asked, a note of desperation in his voice.

Nate's face hardened slightly, the humor fading into a more somber expression. "No, Ethan, nothing. And honestly, part of me wishes it stayed that way. What you did to Ava... it's unforgivable." He paused, collecting his thoughts. "But I'm not just her brother. I'm also your boss. You've been MIA, Ethan. The hospital's buzzing with questions, and I'm running out of plausible excuses for your absence."

Ethan slouched, the weight of Nate's words pressing down on him. "I'm lost, Nate. It's like I'm in this fog, and I can't find my way out," he murmured, his voice barely above a whisper. "Ava's the only one who can clear it, and she's gone. I just... I need to see her, to say I'm sorry, to try and make things right."

Nate's expression softened with sympathy, but he was firm in his response. "Ethan, if I knew where Ava was, I'd tell you. But she didn't say anything to us. It's been a week, and my parents are worried sick."

The room fell silent again, the gravity of the situation settling over them. Ethan's plea hung in the air, unanswered, as he grappled with the reality that Ava had vanished, leaving no trace   behind.

"Look, Ethan, you're a damn good doctor. The hospital needs you, your patients need you. It's not just a job; it's who you are. Don't lose that too," Nate advised, his voice firm yet supportive. "Get back to work. Help those who need you. It's the best distraction, and who knows, it might give you some clarity. Ava... she might need time, but you know her. She's strong, and when she's ready, she'll reach out."

The visit from Nate had offered no solutions, only a reflection of the concern and confusion shared by those who cared about Ava. Ethan was left to confront the hard truth: his actions had not only hurt Ava but had sent ripples of concern and distress through her family as well.

As Nate left, Ethan remained seated, staring into the depths of his untouched coffee, the bitter taste of regret lingering long after the door had closed. His mind raced with thoughts of Ava, her smile, her laughter, the love they had shared, and the future he had recklessly discarded. The realization that he might never get the chance to make amends was a burden he now had to bear, a constant reminder of the love he had lost and   the   pain   he   had   caused.

In the weeks following Ava's departure, Ethan threw himself into his work at the hospital, finding solace in the long hours that kept him from returning to an empty apartment where Ava's absence was a constant, painful reminder.

Violet frequently called him, seeking to reconnect and talk. They hadn't spoken since the day Ava left, and Ethan found himself reluctant to engage. One day, amidst the bustle of the hospital, Ethan heard a familiar voice behind him.

"Ethan..."

Turning around, he found himself face to face with Violet. With a polite but brief excuse to his colleagues, he stepped aside to talk with her.

Ethan sat across from Violet in the hospital cafeteria, the weight of the past few weeks evident in his demeanor. He had been avoiding her calls, not out of anger, but because he wasn't ready to face the consequences of his actions. Violet, however, was persistent.

"I've been calling you, Ethan. Why are you ignoring me?" Violet's voice was tinged with hurt and confusion. "Please, talk to me."

Ethan let out a weary sigh, aware of the few curious glances in their direction. "Vi, you shouldn't have come here. This isn't the right place or time."

Violet's frustration was palpable. "If I didn't come here, would you have continued to ignore me? It's been two weeks, Ethan. I thought you just needed some space, but you never came back to me. What's going on?"

Ethan met her gaze squarely. "Vi, I'm not coming back to you," he said, his voice firm.

Violet's shock was evident. "What do you mean? Is this about feeling guilty for Ava? I can wait, Ethan. You waited six years. This is the least I can do."

Ethan shook his head, the clarity of his decision reflected in his eyes. "No, Vi. It's not about waiting. I don't love you anymore."

Violet stood abruptly, her chair scraping loudly against the floor. "That's impossible, Ethan. You waited for me. You love me."

Ethan's voice was laden with a mixture of remorse and realization as he tried to articulate his feelings to Violet. "Vi, when you came back into my life, it stirred up so many old memories. I thought maybe we could rekindle what we had, that the love I once felt for you was still there. That's why I kept meeting you, even behind Ava's back. I was trying to grasp something from our past, something I thought was still alive."

He paused, his gaze distant, reflecting on the painful journey. "But then, when Ava saw us together, when you kissed me, the look of utter heartbreak on her face... It was a moment of painful clarity for me. I saw the depth of her love and the magnitude of the pain I was causing her. In trying to recapture the past with you, I was destroying the most precious thing in my present."

Violet's face contorted with anger and disbelief. "So what? Ava's pain made you realize you don't love me? That's ridiculous, Ethan! You waited for me, you wanted me back!"

Ethan looked at her, his eyes filled with a sorrowful understanding. "I thought I did, Vi. I really thought I did. But seeing Ava in so much pain made me realize something crucial – I couldn't bear to lose her. It made me see that what I felt for you was anchored in the past, not in where I am now, not in who I've become."

Violet shook her head vehemently, refusing to accept his words. "No, Ethan. This is just guilt talking. You love me; I know you do. Ava just manipulated you into feeling this way."

Ethan's response was quiet but firm. "It's not guilt, Vi. It's realization. Ava never manipulated me. I hurt her deeply, and in doing so, I've come to see where my heart truly lies. With Ava, I found a love that grew and evolved over time. I just didn't see it until it was too late."

"Am I supposed to forget that nothing happened between us these past weeks, Ethan?" Violet's frustration stiffened her expression.

Ethan let out a deep sigh and met her gaze. "Vi, the truth is, nothing really happened between us, except for that one day when Ava saw us kiss," he admitted, his voice tinged with guilt over the incident. "I thought I wanted to be with you during these past few days, but I've come to realize that it was more of a remnant of my past feelings for you. I was overwhelmed in the moment when you first came back, and I said things I thought I meant, but now I see it differently."

Violet, her anger boiling over, stood up abruptly. "So, I lose to Ava again? Because she got to you first this time?"

Ethan's voice carried a depth of understanding that he had only recently come to grips with. "It's not about winning or losing, Vi. It's about recognizing where my heart truly belongs. And I'm sorry, but it doesn't belong with you anymore," he said, a heavy sigh punctuating his words.

As Violet reacted with anger and disbelief, Ethan saw, perhaps for the first time, the true nature of her feelings. It wasn't just about love; it was about competition, about winning something she thought was rightfully hers. He remembered how, back in college, Violet had always been in a silent rivalry with Ava, constantly trying to outdo her in every aspect, whether it was grades or social standing. And now, he realized, he was just another one of those things she wanted to win over Ava.

"Ethan, you can't do this to me. You waited for me. You wanted to be with me," Violet argued, her frustration evident.

Ethan looked at her, finally seeing the situation for what it really was. "Vi, I'm realizing now that you never really wanted me for me. It was always about Ava, wasn't it? In college, you were always trying to compete with her, to prove that you could have anything she could. I was just a part of that competition."

Violet faltered for a moment, her façade cracking under the weight of his words.

He continued, more to himself than to her, "All this time, I thought we had something special. But it's clear now that it was never about love. It was about winning against Ava. And I... I got caught up in that without even realizing it."

Violet, unable to counter his realization, stormed out of the cafeteria, leaving Ethan alone with his thoughts. He sat there, grappling with the painful truth that had unfolded before him. His relationship with Violet had been built on a foundation of rivalry and competition, not genuine love.

As he sat in the empty cafeteria, Ethan's heart ached for Ava. He had let himself be a pawn in Violet's game, and in doing so, he had lost the one person who truly loved him for who he was. The regret of his actions and the loss of Ava weighed heavily on him, a burden he would carry with him as he faced a future without her.

Just as Ethan was about to seek a moment of respite in the residents' lounge, a brief escape from the day's turmoil, his colleague intercepted him with a message that demanded his immediate attention. "Ethan, the chief of surgery is asking for you," his colleague informed him, the urgency in their voice cutting through Ethan's fatigue.

Taking a deep breath to steady his nerves, Ethan knocked and entered, ready to face whatever awaited him. Ethan sat rigidly in the chief of surgery's office, his father across from him. The air was tense, laden with unspoken words. Dr. Williams, Ethan's father, broke the silence, his voice a blend of relief and concern. "Ethan, it's good to see you back at work. How have you been holding up?"

Before Ethan could muster a response, his father continued, addressing the elephant in the room. "I was informed you were seen in the cafeteria with a woman. That was Violet, wasn't it?" his father inquired, his tone suggesting it was more a statement than a question. "Ethan, don't you think distancing yourself from her would be wise under the circumstances? After all, her involvement is what led to your split with Ava. And honestly, it's time to let go of the past, especially considering Violet left six years ago."

The mention of Violet ignited a fury in Ethan, his pent-up emotions finding an outlet. "Do you know why Violet left, Dad? Because you threatened her! You said you'd ruin her life, pull her scholarship, blacklist her from hospitals in the States!"

Dr. Williams' expression registered shock, a mix of confusion and disbelief. "Ethan, I did speak to Violet, but I never threatened her. I wanted her away from you, yes, but not through threats."

The room's atmosphere shifted as Dr. Williams divulged the painful truth. "I saw Violet for what she truly was – a woman more in love with our family's wealth and connections than with you. I offered her money to leave you, any amount she wanted. She didn't hesitate, Ethan. She took the money and left the very next day."

Ethan's world seemed to crumble around him as he absorbed the revelation. The woman he'd once loved, the memories they shared, all tainted by the truth of her betrayal. "Why... why didn't you tell me, Dad?" Ethan's voice was a fragile whisper, barely concealing his profound sense of betrayal.

Dr. Williams' gaze softened, tinged with regret. "I thought it didn't matter. I wanted to spare you the additional pain. And when you started dating Ava, I saw how happy she made you. I let it go, believing it was best left in the past."

Ethan's world seemed to shatter into a million pieces as his father's words sank in. The hurt, the bitter taste of betrayal, and the sting of lost love hit him all at once. He realized he'd lost Ava, the one person who had truly loved him, because of a lie, a mirage of a past love that was never real.

The room started to close in on him as the enormity of what he'd done, the missed chances, and the brutal truth weighed him down. He felt the full, crushing impact of losing Ava, a future that could have been, now broken because of decisions made in the shadows of a past that was nothing but a facade. In that moment, Ethan understood, painfully so, how the past, no matter how much it hurts, steers the choices we make and the path our life takes.

CHAPTER FIFTEEN

"Mom, I'm okay where I am right now. You don't have to worry about me," Ava assured her mother over the phone. It had been two months since she had made the difficult decision to leave home after the heartbreaking end of her relationship with Ethan. Although she regularly called to reassure her mother of her well-being, Ava wasn't yet ready to reveal her whereabouts.

A heavy sigh came through the line. "Can you just tell us what really happened, darling? Ethan told us it was his fault that the wedding was called off. Did he... Did he really cheat on you with Violet?" Her mother's disbelief was palpable, her voice laced with a mixture of shock and denial.

Ava's heart skipped a beat. "How... how did you find out, Mom?"

The line crackled softly as her mother replied, "Ethan visited us the day you left and confessed everything. But, Ava, why didn't you come to us? We're your family. We're meant to support each other. The thought of you dealing with this pain all by yourself is unbearable. I should've been there for you through all of this," her mother's voice broke, overcome with emotion.

Tears streamed down Ava's cheeks, the sound of her mother's sobs echoing her own heartache. "I'm so... sorry, Mommy. I just... I didn't know how to face anyone. I was so embarrassed and hurt. I felt so betrayed, so lost. I needed time to just be by myself, to make sense of everything."

Her mother's voice softened. "Honey, there's nothing to be embarrassed about. You did nothing wrong. Ethan made a mistake, not you. And you don't have to go through this alone. We are your family, Ava. We love you no matter what."

Ava clenched the phone tighter, feeling the chasm of physical distance that lay between her and the comforting embrace she longed for. "I know, Mom, and I can't tell you how much that means to me. But I'm just not ready to come back yet. There's something inside me that I need to find, some strength or peace, I guess. I promise I won't be gone forever. I just need a little more time."

There was a pause, and Ava could picture her mother nodding in understanding, even with a heavy heart. "Okay, darling. I won't force you. But please, don't shut us out. We're here for you whenever you're ready. Your father and I, we worry about you every single day."

Ava felt a lump in her throat. "I promise, I'll keep calling. And... maybe soon, I'll be ready to come home. Just not yet."

Her mother sighed, the sound carrying years of love and worry. "Alright. Just remember, our door is always open, and our hearts are always with you, wherever you are. We love you so much, Ava."

"I love you, Mom. Thank you for being there, even when I'm so far away," Ava whispered, the words mingling with her tears, a testament to the unbreakable bond that distance could never sever. They shared a few more words, a delicate dance of comfort and love, before the call ended, leaving Ava with a heart heavy with sorrow but warmed by the undying love of her family.

The room was silent except for the soft ticking of the wall clock, the sound oddly magnified in the tense atmosphere. Ava sat rigidly in the plush chair, her fingers still entwined around her phone, the final words of her mother echoing in her heart, a distant yet comforting melody. As she gently ended the call, a sense of solitude enveloped her, the room feeling larger and more imposing than before.

The door creaked open, breaking the stillness, and the doctor, a kind-faced woman with gentle eyes, stepped in, holding a clipboard close to her chest. The contrast between the warmth of her mother's distant support and the clinical, impersonal setting of the doctor's office was stark, amplifying the whirlwind of emotions swirling within Ava.

"Ava," the doctor began, her voice soft yet clear, "the test results are in, and it's confirmed. You are eight weeks pregnant."

The words hung heavily in the air, resonating with a gravity that seemed to pull Ava into a moment of profound realization. Her mind raced back to that fateful night with Ethan, a memory painted with shades of tenderness and vulnerability, now forever altered by the unfolding reality. She remembered the warmth of Ethan's embrace, a stark contrast to the cold, sterile room she now found herself in.

The doctor misread the silence, her professional demeanor masking a hint of concern. "Ava, I understand this may come as a shock. You have options. If you're considering terminating the pregnancy, we can make arrangements for the procedure today."

The mention of 'options' jolted Ava back to the present. Her hand instinctively caressed her abdomen, a protective gesture that was both reflexive and tender. The notion of a life, a tiny, innocent being growing inside her, ignited a fierce determination she didn't know she possessed. Tears welled up in her eyes, not from despair, but from a sudden, overwhelming sense of love and responsibility.

"No," Ava's voice was a mere whisper, yet it carried the weight of her resolve. "No, I'm keeping the baby. I may be alone, and this... this wasn't planned. But this child... this child is a part of me. I'll do whatever it takes to be a good mother."

The doctor regarded her with a newfound respect, the professional barrier giving way to genuine empathy. "Ava, this journey won't be easy, but you won't be alone. We'll provide all the support and care you need. This is your choice, and we're here to help you through it."

As Ava left the clinic, the realization of her new reality began to sink in. Yes, the road ahead was uncertain and undoubtedly filled with challenges. But in her heart, a fierce love was taking root, a love that promised to be her strength, her beacon, guiding her through the storms to come. She was a mother, a protector, a provider. And in that moment, despite the chaos of her world, Ava felt a profound sense of peace. She was not alone – she had a purpose, a tiny, yet immensely powerful reason to face each day with courage and hope.

Months had swiftly transitioned into seasons, each day bringing Ava closer to the life burgeoning within her. The sting of betrayal from Ethan and Violet's actions lingered like a distant echo, but Ava had cocooned herself in a sanctuary of resilience and hope for the new life she carried. Her focus was unwavering: to nurture and protect the tiny heartbeat that had become her world.

Ava had chosen to keep her pregnancy a secret from her family, not out of fear or shame, but from a deep-rooted desire to present them with a fait accompli. She wanted to heal, to stand strong as a mother before reintroducing herself to her family in this new role, to show them her strength and the new life she had embraced wholeheartedly.

Now, seven months after learning she was pregnant, Ava's world was a symphony of anticipation and preparation. Her days in Ketchikan were quiet yet busy, filled with the tender routines of expectant motherhood. Today, she was strolling through downtown, her list of essentials for the baby fluttering in her hand like a tangible piece of her growing excitement.

"Ava? Ava, is that you?" The voice cut through the hum of the downtown buzz, familiar yet misplaced in the context of her new life.

Turning, Ava's eyes met with a figure from a chapter of her life that seemed like a distant memory. "Brian?" she uttered, her mind piecing together the friendly bar owner she had met in New York.

Brian's smile was warm, but his eyes quickly widened in surprise as they landed on her pronounced belly. "Wow, Ava, congratulations! I had no idea. Everything turned out well, I see! How's your fiancé? Or is he your husband now? He must be thrilled," he said, the words tumbling out in a cheerful rush.

The mention of Ethan cast a shadow across Ava's features, a brief cloud of pain that she swiftly pushed aside. "Ethan and I, we're not together anymore. It's just me and my little one now," she said, her voice carrying a tremble of resolve.

Before Brian could respond, a sudden sharp sensation took Ava by surprise. Her breath hitched, her hands instinctively cradling her belly. "Oh no, Brian, I think... I think it's time."

Brian's expression shifted from surprise to immediate concern. "Ava, don't worry, I've got you," he said firmly, guiding her gently to a nearby bench. His hands were steady as he took out his phone, dialing for an ambulance with practiced calm. "Stay with me, Ava. Help is on the way. You're going to be fine, and so is your baby."

Ava nodded, trying to steady her breathing, her mind a whirlwind of fear and anticipation. "Thank you, Brian. I didn't expect... I mean, I can't believe this is happening now."

"Hey, life has a funny way of surprising us, doesn't it? But you're not alone, Ava. I'm here, and I'll stay with you until help arrives. You're strong, and you're going to get through this," Brian reassured her, his presence a steady anchor in the storm of sudden onset labor.

As the sound of sirens approached, signaling the arrival of the ambulance, Ava grasped Brian's hand, a silent thank you in her grip. Today, a new chapter was about to begin, and despite the swirling uncertainty and the pain of the past, Ava knew she was ready to embrace the future, to welcome the new life she had so lovingly prepared for.

After a grueling thirty-hour labor that tested the limits of her endurance, Ava was rewarded with the most precious gift – her beautiful baby girl, Lily. The first time the nurse gently placed Lily in her arms, Ava felt a sense of completeness, a profound connection that words could never fully capture.

Every pain, every struggle seemed to dissolve in the presence of this tiny, perfect life she had brought into the world.

Ava was gently roused from her rest by the soft creak of the door opening. Her eyes fluttered open to see a nurse, her smile as warm as the morning sun, stepping into the room. "Good morning, Mrs. Greenwood. Your husband is here to see you," the nurse announced, her voice cheerful as she held the door open.

Ava's heart skipped a beat. 'Husband? It can't be... Ethan doesn't even know.' Confusion clouded her thoughts until she saw who it was. Brian, the bar owner from New York, stood in the doorway, his arms laden with a vibrant bouquet of roses and a basket brimming with fresh fruits.

"Hey there!" Brian greeted her with his characteristic warmth, his eyes immediately drawn to her significant transformation. The nurse excused herself after a brief check on Ava's IV fluids.

Ava offered a smile, tinged with a complexity of emotions. "Brian, I didn't expect... I mean, I thought you might have left already."

He chuckled, the sound a soothing balm to the sterile hospital environment. "Leave? And miss the chance to celebrate this moment with you? No way. Besides, I couldn't bear the thought of you being here all by yourself." He handed her the bouquet. "Congratulations, Ava. Lily is absolutely beautiful, just like her mother."

Ava's eyes glistened, the gesture touching a chord deep within her. "Thank you, Brian. You've been more than kind. But you really should get some rest.

You've been here since I was admitted. I don't want to be a burden."

Brian's reply was swift and sincere. "It's no burden. I want to be here." He paused, his tone shifting slightly. "Have you had the chance to call your family or... Ethan?" he asked tentatively.

Ava slowly shook her head. "I'll call my parents later. I just need a moment to gather my strength." She offered a weak smile, the physical and emotional toll of the birth still lingering.

After a short silence, she continued, her voice barely above a whisper. "Ethan... he doesn't need to know. Lily and I, we're going to make it on our own. He's moved on with his life, and it's time I do the same."

Brian's smile was one of quiet understanding as he took a seat beside her bed. "I'll stay then, at least until your family arrives. You shouldn't be alone right now, not with a newborn to care for. And hey, I'm pretty good with babies," he added, his laughter softening the gravity of the moment.

Ava's resistance faded into a grateful smile. "Why are you in Alaska, anyway? Just visiting?"

Brian began peeling an apple from the fruit basket. "Actually, I'm from Ketchikan. It's been a few years since I was last here. Came back for my sister's wedding."

"And are you heading back to New York soon?" Ava inquired, curiosity tinting her voice.

He glanced at her, a knowing smile playing on his lips. "I might stick around a little longer. Seems I've found a reason to stay."

The conversation was gently interrupted by a knock and the nurse re-entering, pushing a bassinet. Ava's heart melted at the sight of Lily, peacefully resting.

"It's time for her feeding," the nurse said, expertly placing Lily in Ava's arms.

Cradling her daughter, Ava whispered softly, "Hey, sweetheart... I've missed you." The tender moment was amplified when Lily's tiny hand wrapped around Ava's finger.

Brian watched, a smile of admiration on his face. Ava, radiant and full of love, seemed to glow in the presence of her child.

Noticing the time for privacy, Brian stood. "I guess it's time for me to step out. I'll be back later. Here's my number if you need anything," he said, placing a card on the table.

"Thank you, Brian," Ava responded, her attention now fully on Lily.

With a soft chuckle, Brian exited the room, leaving mother and daughter to their sacred moment of bonding. Ava, filled with love and determination, turned her full attention to Lily, ready to embark on the journey of motherhood, her heart swelling with a love she never knew possible.

A month after Ava and her newborn daughter, Lily, were discharged from the hospital, Ava mustered the courage to make an important call. Picking up her phone, she dialed her parents' number, her heart pounding with a mix of nervousness and anticipation.

"Mom, Dad, it's me, Ava," she began, her voice trembling slightly. "I'm in Ketchikan, Alaska. There's something... something very important I need to tell you. But I can't say it over the phone. Can you come here?"

There was a pause, filled with concern and confusion. "Ava, darling, are you alright? What's going on?" her mother's voice was laced with worry.

"I'm okay, Mom. I just really need you to be here. It's something I have to show you," Ava insisted, her voice steadying with resolve.

"We'll be on the next flight out," her father assured her, his tone firm and protective.

The next day, Ava waited anxiously in the lavish lobby of the penthouse hotel. Her heart skipped a beat as she spotted her family walking through the entrance. She rushed towards them, her emotions spilling over.

"Mom! Dad! Nate!" she exclaimed, tears already streaming down her face.

"Ava, my baby girl, we've been so worried about you," her mother murmured, holding her at arm's length to take a better look at her. "But you look... you look well, thank God."

Pulling back slightly, Ava looked at each of their faces, her heart swelling with love. "I've missed you all so much. I'm sorry for worrying you."

Her father, his eyes glistening with unshed tears, spoke softly, "You're our daughter, Ava. We just want to make sure you're safe."

Nate, his curiosity piqued, asked, "So, what's this all about, little sis? You mentioned something important on the phone."

Ava met their concerned gazes, her heart swelling with a cocktail of emotions. "I... I have something to show you, something really important. But not here, in the lobby. Let's go up to my room. Please."

With puzzled looks, her family nodded, and they all moved toward the elevator. The ride up was quiet, the air thick with anticipation. Ava's mind raced with a thousand scenarios, but she held onto the certainty that, no matter what, her family's love was unwavering.

Stepping into the plush living room of her suite, Ava's family took in the luxurious surroundings, their curiosity growing by the second. Ava's family was surprised to see a man waiting inside. Ava hesitated for a moment, then spoke.

"Everyone, this is Brian. He's a friend who has been helping me a lot here," Ava introduced.

Brian stood up and extended his hand in greeting. "It's a pleasure to meet you all. Ava's told me so much about you."

After brief introductions and handshakes, Ava excused herself. "I'll be just a moment," she said, her voice filled with a mix of nerves and excitement.

Her family waited in the living room, exchanging curious glances and small talk with Brian, who answered their questions with a friendly but guarded demeanor.

"What do you think it is?" Nate's voice was low but carried his typical concern.

"I don't know, but she seems different. Calmer, somehow," her father mused, his analytical mind at work.

Her mother, more emotional, added, "She's hiding something, but I can sense it's not bad. Just... unexpected."

The door opened again, and Ava reappeared, this time not alone. In her arms, she carried the most precious part of her life, her daughter Lily. The room fell into a stunned silence, each family member trying to comprehend the sight before them.

"Ava, who..." her mother's voice trailed off, unable to finish the question.

Ava took a deep breath, her eyes shining with unshed tears. "Mom, Dad, Nate... meet Lily. She's my daughter, your granddaughter, your niece. She's... she's Ethan's too."

A gasp rippled through the room, a wave of shock, confusion, and then, slowly, understanding.

Her mother stepped forward, her hands trembling as she reached out to touch Lily's tiny hand. "She's beautiful, Ava... she's perfect."

Her father, a silent strength beside her, wrapped an arm around her mother. "Ava, why didn't you tell us? You shouldn't have gone through this alone."

Nate, always quick to react, was at her side in an instant. "I can't believe it... I'm an uncle? She's adorable, Ava."

Ava's smile was a mix of relief and love. "I wanted to tell you in person. I wanted you to meet her and see that... that we're okay. Lily is the best thing that's ever happened to me. And Brian... he's been a great friend through all this."

The room was filled with a new energy, a mix of astonishment, joy, and the immediate love that only family can bring. Questions, laughter, and cooing over Lily filled the space, each member of the family drawn to the tiny life that had brought them all together in this unexpected, beautiful way.

As the evening progressed, the warmth of family filled the living room, creating a cocoon of comfort and nostalgia. After the remnants of dinner had been cleared away, Ava found herself nestled between her parents on the plush sofa, the familiar closeness bringing both comfort and a surge of emotions.

"Ava, honey," her father began, his voice layered with a gentle firmness as he held her hand, "I think it's time for you to consider coming home. Especially now that you have Lily in your life. We've missed you immensely."

Her mother chimed in, her words echoing the sentiment. "That's right, darling. We want both of you to be within arm's reach, always. Alaska might as well be another world away from New York."

Ava's heart was a turmoil of conflicting emotions, and her hesitation was palpable. "Mom, Dad... I'm just not sure going back is the right move for me... for Lily," she said, her voice tinged with a sorrowful undertone.

Her mother's intuition kicked in, her voice softening as she probed deeper. "Is this about Ethan, honey?" Ava's silence was answer enough, prompting her mother to continue, "Don't you think he deserves to know about Lily? After all, he is her father."

The protective shield around Ava's resolve wavered. "Lily is mine," she asserted, a hint of steel woven into her trembling voice. "I'm not part of his world anymore, and I don't want Lily to be just some obligation for him. He's got his life sorted with Violet. Bringing Lily into that would only complicate things, make him feel trapped. He'd do what he thinks he should, not what he wants."

Nate, with a tone suggesting he knew more, cautiously interjected, "But Ava, you might not know this, Ethan and Violet have—"

Ava's voice, firm and resolute, cut through his attempt. "I don't want to hear about it, Nate. That part of my life, it's over. My entire focus, every bit of energy and love I have, it's for Lily now," her voice trembled, betraying the pain behind her words. "Please, just promise me none of you will tell Ethan about us. He's chosen his path. Lily and I, we'll make our own way."

Her tears, no longer held back, cascaded down her cheeks, each one a silent testament to her resolve and her heartache. "I'm rebuilding, bit by bit, with Lily. She's my world now," she sobbed, the weight of her journey pressing down on her.

In that moment, her mother's arms wrapped around her, offering a safe harbor from the storm of her emotions. Her father's hand on her back provided a steady, comforting presence.

In the midst of this family tableau, Brian stood by the window, a silent observer. His heart ached for Ava; her strength and vulnerability resonated with him on a level he hadn't anticipated.

The sound of Lily's cry broke the heavy atmosphere. Ava made to stand, but Brian's calm voice interjected. "Let me check on her, Ava. You stay here with your family."

Moments after Brian disappeared into the bedroom with Lily, the sound of her cries faded away. When he reemerged, cradling Lily in his arms, the baby's face was aglow with a contented calm. "Looks like our little princess just needed a bit of comforting," Brian chuckled warmly.

"I can see Lily's quite comfortable with you, Brian," Ava's father noted with a warm smile.

Standing up and wiping away the last of her tears, Ava replied with a gentle smile, "She is, Dad. Brian has a way with her. It's like she knows she's safe when he's holding her."

Nate, with a playful grin, chimed in, "Seems like Lily's already figured out how to get everyone wrapped around her little finger."

Ava's mother approached, her grandmother's heart alight with joy and wonder. "Look at her, dozing off again. She's so peaceful with you, Brian. Thank you for being so gentle and caring with her," she expressed sincerely.

Brian responded with a genuine smile. "It's an absolute joy. She is a wonderful little girl," he replied, his affection for the child evident in his voice. Nate noticed the tenderness in Brian's actions and the care in his words. He caught a subtle warmth in Brian's demeanor toward Ava, a silent, caring presence that didn't go unnoticed. Nate chose to keep this observation to himself, a knowing look flickering in his eyes.

The room was filled with a comfortable warmth as Ava's father took a moment to address a more practical matter. "Ava, while it's great to see how well you're managing here, a hotel isn't a home. You and Lily deserve a proper place, a space where you both can truly settle."

Ava nodded, understanding the weight of his words. "I've been thinking about that, Dad. Just haven't found the right place yet."

With a reassuring squeeze of her hand, her father replied, "Leave that to me. I'll find you a property by tomorrow. Consider it a new beginning for you and Lily—a gift from us to you both."

Ava's eyes filled with gratitude and a touch of surprise. "Dad, that's... thank you, really. I don't know what to say," she murmured, her voice a mix of emotion and heartfelt appreciation as she leaned into the comforting embrace of her family, the future looking a little brighter with their support and love.

CHAPTER SIXTEEN

The sound of Lily's joyful voice brought a warmth to the cozy patisserie shop that Ava had carefully nurtured in Ketchikan, Alaska. "Mommy! Mommy!" Lily's excitement was infectious, and customers couldn't help but smile at the adorable sight.

Ava scooped up her daughter, a tender smile playing on her lips. "Hi baby... Remember, we don't run inside the shop, okay?" she gently reminded her.

Lily, her eyes shining with mischief, playfully covered her mouth with her tiny hand. "Opsie... I just missed you so very much, Mommy!"

Ava kissed her daughter's forehead, her heart swelling with love. "And I missed you too, my little Lily," she whispered.

In Ketchikan, Ava had poured her heart into creating 'Lily's Flour Garden', a charming patisserie nestled beneath their home. It was a smaller, more intimate version of her successful

'La Belle Époque Patisserie' chain, which she had left under the capable management of her mother. Here, in this quiet corner of Alaska, she found peace and purpose, balancing her roles as a business owner and a loving mother.

Each day in the patisserie was a blend of sweet aromas, the laughter of her daughter, and the contentment of a life she had bravely built on her own terms.

Inside Lily's Flour Garden, the cozy patisserie was buzzing with the gentle hum of satisfied customers and the sweet aroma of freshly baked treats. Ava, with her usual grace and efficiency, moved behind the counter, serving customers with a warm smile. In a corner table close to the counter, little Lily was seated, deeply engrossed in coloring her favorite book, her crayons spread out around her.

A young woman, holding a steaming cup of coffee and a croissant, approached Ava at the counter. "Your patisserie is just wonderful," she began, her eyes glancing over at Lily. "And your little girl, she's adorable. Is she your daughter?"

Ava glanced at Lily and smiled proudly. "Yes, that's Lily. She's my world. Thank you for your kind words."

The woman smiled back, watching Lily. "She seems so happy here, coloring away. You've created such a lovely, welcoming place."

As Ava prepared the woman's order, another customer, a regular who had been coming since the patisserie opened, joined in the conversation. "Ava, your shop has become a staple in Ketchikan. It's not just the delicious pastries, but the warmth and love you put into this place. And Lily, she's like the little mascot of your shop!"

Ava laughed, her heart swelling with happiness. "Thank you. It's been a dream to run this place, and having Lily here makes it even more special."

As the afternoon progressed, more customers came in, some regulars, some new, all greeted by the charming sight of Lily and the enticing smells of the patisserie. Ava moved around, chatting with customers, taking orders, and at times glancing over at Lily, ensuring she was content.

"Mommy, look!" Lily's voice, bright with pride, cut through the hum of conversations. She held up her coloring book, showcasing a meticulously colored flower.

Ava paused, her heart swelling at the sight. "That's beautiful, sweetheart!" she praised, leaning down to envelop Lily in a quick, warm hug. "You're quite the artist."

Their interaction didn't go unnoticed. Customers nearby couldn't help but admire the warm mother-daughter moment, some remarking on the family-like atmosphere Ava had cultivated in her patisserie.

The cozy ambiance was momentarily filled with Lily's excited voice. "I can't wait to show this to Daddy Brian! When is he coming back, mommy?"

Brian, a constant, loving presence in their lives, had returned to New York a week ago to tend to his club but was never far from Lily's thoughts. Over the years, Brian's bond with Lily had deepened, naturally evolving to the point where Lily affectionately referred to him as 'Daddy Brian,' a title that held a special place in Brian's heart.

Ava had once apologized to Brian for the informal title, wary of overstepping boundaries, but to her relief, Brian cherished it. His bond with Lily was something pure and genuine, a relationship that had grown organically and become a cornerstone of their lives.

"He'll be back soon, sweetie. In about three days, I think. Didn't he mention when he'd return? I thought you two shared everything," Ava teased, her tone light and playful.

Lily let out a dramatic sigh, her childlike impatience endearing. "Nope, he didn't say. I'm gonna be so mad at him if he doesn't come back soon!" she declared, her words carrying the weight of a child's earnestness before she turned her attention back to her coloring.

Ava couldn't help but smile at her daughter's words. Brian's influence on Lily was undeniable; he had become an indispensable part of their family.

As the day's light began to fade, marking the end of another bustling afternoon at the patisserie, Ava reached for the sign on the door, ready to flip it to 'Closed.' But the gentle tinkle of the bell halted her mid-motion. As she turned, her prepared words of apology for the late customer caught in her throat. It wasn't just any customer; it was Brian, and the sight of him was like a familiar melody that still managed to surprise her heart each time.

Time had indeed been a craftsman in shaping Brian. The years had refined his features, lending a rugged edge to his charm. He stood there, casually clad in a simple, snug-fitting shirt that subtly hinted at the strength underneath, and jeans that seemed tailor-made for him. The ensemble was effortless, yet it spoke volumes of a man who carried a natural, understated confidence.

"Hi, surprise!" His voice was a warm, welcoming embrace all on its own. The lopsided grin that accompanied his greeting was enough to light up the room, a playful spark dancing in his eyes. He carried a colorful array of gift bags and a bouquet of tulips, their hues vibrant against the cozy backdrop of the patisserie. Without hesitation, he bridged the gap between them, wrapping Ava in a hug that felt like a long-awaited reunion. "I've missed you," he murmured, the words resonating with a depth of feeling that tugged at something deep within her.

For a moment, Ava was caught off guard, her heart fluttering in an unexpected rhythm. But as she eased into the embrace, a soft chuckle escaped her lips. "Bri, you're full of surprises. Lily's been counting the days till you're back," she replied, her voice a mix of affection and mild reproof for his unannounced return.

Brian gently pulled away, his hands presenting her with the tulips, his gaze holding hers in a silent conversation. "Just Lily? I was hoping you'd be a bit happy to see me too," he teased, the mischievous glint in his eyes softening into something more tender, more vulnerable.

Ava knew their friendship had always been laced with an undercurrent of unspoken emotions. Brian had never been overt about his feelings, respecting her need to focus on Lily and rebuild her life. But his actions, often more telling than words, hinted at a deeper affection, like the tender hug and the heartfelt admission of missing her.

"Would you like to see Lily now, or should we go upstairs? She's just in the living room watching her favorite shows," Ava suggested, gently steering the conversation, even as she acknowledged the familiar flutter in her heart.

"Let's stay here for a moment. There's something I want to talk to you about..." Brian's voice took on a serious note, causing a flicker of anxiety to pass through Ava.

"Of course, let's sit down over here," she said, motioning towards a cozy corner table.

As they settled in, Brian's demeanor revealed a mix of nerves and resolve. He took a deep breath, gathering his thoughts before meeting Ava's gaze, his eyes a clear window to his soul.

"Ava," he began, his voice a low, earnest timbre that commanded the space between them, "there's something I've been holding inside for a long time, and I think it's time you knew the truth of it." His eyes met hers, unflinching and intense, a clear window into the depth of what he was about to reveal.

"From the moment you walked into my club years ago, there was something about you that captivated me. It wasn't just your beauty or the strength I saw in you; it was the way you carried your pain, yet still managed to smile, to be kind, to be you. And when our paths crossed again here in Ketchikan, that feeling didn't just return—it grew, it deepened."

Ava listened, her heart in her throat, her breath a silent captive to the confession unfolding before her.

"It was the way you embraced motherhood with Lily, the way you've been everything she needed and more, that showed me just how incredible you truly are. And somewhere along the way, that admiration, that respect, it transformed into something more—something deeper and undeniable."

Brian's voice was a steady stream, each word deliberate, each pause heavy with emotion. "I've loved you, Ava. Silently, from a distance, because I knew the timing wasn't right. You were healing, you were building a life for you and Lily, and I never wanted to be anything but a support to you in that journey. But now, here, in this quiet corner of our world, I can't hide what's in my heart any longer. I love you, Ava. I love Lily as if she were my own. I'm not asking for an immediate answer or for you to change anything about the beautiful life you've built. All I'm asking is for a chance. A chance to show you the depth of my feelings, to prove that happiness, our happiness, is something worth exploring, worth cherishing."

As Brian's heartfelt declaration settled into the space between them, Ava felt her heart pounding with an intensity that left her momentarily lost for words. His gaze, so full of sincerity and hope, seemed to pierce right through the walls she had meticulously built around her heart.

Finally, she found her voice, albeit a soft, uncertain whisper. "Brian, this is... it's a lot to take in. It's been so long since anyone has opened their heart to me like this. The last time was with Ethan, and that feels like a lifetime ago."

She took a deep breath, her eyes meeting his, a torrent of emotions swirling within. "I'm not hesitating because of Ethan. He's a part of my past, and that's where he'll stay. But Brian, I'm scared. Scared of diving into something new, of taking a chance on love again. If I let you closer, I can't make any promises. I can't promise that I'll want to date or that my feelings will align with yours. And this is something I need to think through deeply, especially because you're not just anyone. You've been such an important part of our lives, mine and Lily's. The last thing I would ever want is to hurt you or to take your feelings lightly."

Brian listened intently, his expression one of understanding and acceptance. After she finished, he gently reached for her hand, his touch reassuring. "Ava, I'm not asking for promises or instant decisions. All I'm asking for is a chance to show you how much you and Lily mean to me. If all you're ready for now is to consider the possibility of us, then I'm here for that. I'll be here, and we can take this as slowly as you need."

The honesty and patience in his words touched a chord within Ava, stirring a warmth that she hadn't realized was there. A part of her, a part that she had guarded so fiercely, seemed to resonate with his gentle, unwavering presence.

"Okay, Brian," she said, a small, tentative smile forming on her lips. "I hear you. And... and I'm open to seeing where this goes, at our own pace. Slowly."

Brian's response was a smile that seemed to light up the entire room, his eyes reflecting a quiet joy. "Slowly it is," he agreed, his hand still holding hers, a simple yet profound connection in the midst of life's complexities.

In the soft glow of the patisserie, as the day outside came to a gentle close, a subtle shift had occurred. It was a shift not of grand declarations or sudden changes, but of quiet acknowledgments and the gentle uncurling of hearts, ready to explore the tender nuances of growing affection and the possibility of new beginnings.

The sun was high and bright, casting a cheerful glow over the amusement park as Brian, Ava, and Lily made their way through the bustling crowds. Lily's excitement was palpable, her hand firmly grasped in Brian's as they navigated the colorful maze of attractions.

"Look at that, Lily! How about we kick things off with the Ferris wheel? You can see the whole park from up there!" Brian suggested, his voice infused with excitement, perfectly in tune with Lily's bubbling enthusiasm.

Lily's response was a vigorous nod, her other hand tugging at Ava's. "Yes, let's go, Mommy! I want to see everything!"

As they approached the ride, Lily's small steps quickened, her eagerness barely contained. Noticing her struggle to keep up, Brian scooped her up onto his shoulders with an effortless grace. "Up you go, champ! You'll get the royal view from up here!" he exclaimed, earning a delighted squeal from Lily.

Ava's heart swelled at the sight. "You two are quite the pair," she remarked, her voice laced with affection.

Brian flashed a warm smile. "We make a great team, don't we, Lily?"

"The best team!" Lily chimed in, her hands playfully patting Brian's head.

The day unfolded like a vibrant tapestry of laughter and shared joy. At every turn, Brian's attentiveness shone through. Whenever Lily's gaze lingered on a fluffy toy or her nose twitched at the scent of popcorn, Brian was quick to notice.

"Lily, those stuffed animals look pretty cool. Want to win one?" he asked, his eyes twinkling with the challenge.

Lily's enthusiastic agreement led them to a game booth, where Brian skillfully tossed rings and knocked down targets, much to the delight of his cheering squad. "Daddy Brian, you did it!" Lily's cheer filled the air as Brian handed her a giant stuffed bear, a trophy of their fun-filled conquest.

As they ventured from ride to ride, their laughter mingled with the melodic backdrop of the amusement park. They twirled in teacups, made a splash on the log flume, and danced with the breeze on the swing carousel, each moment a precious snapshot of happiness.

Taking a momentary break on a nearby bench, Lily hugged her new bear tight, her face the picture of contentment. Brian turned to Ava, his voice carrying a heartfelt sincerity. "Seeing her this joyful, it's what makes days like this so special. It's all about these moments, Ava."

Ava met his gaze, the depth of her gratitude mirrored in her eyes. "Brian, I can't even begin to express how much this means to us. You've brought so much light into our lives. Lily adores you, and... so do I," she confessed, the words spoken with a gentle honesty.

As Brian gently took Ava's hand, his touch conveyed not just affection, but a profound sense of gratitude and happiness. He wanted her to know how much her words, her acknowledgment of his role in their lives, truly meant to him. Ava had noticed, ever since Brian had begun his thoughtful courtship, how he seamlessly wove his way into their daily lives. Not a day passed without a sweet gesture from him, be it a bouquet of her favorite flowers or a thoughtful note. But what really touched Ava's heart was his genuine inclusion of Lily in every plan, every date, every moment they shared.

Catching Ava's smile as he held her hand, Brian couldn't help but reflect it back, his own expression warm and content. In that moment, with Lily perched happily on his shoulders and Ava's hand in his, they truly resembled the picture of a perfect, joyful family.

The energy of the day only escalated as they made their way to the pirate ship ride. They settled in, Lily snugly positioned between Brian and Ava. The anticipation built as the ship began its ascent, and then, with each thrilling drop, their laughter and screams merged with those of the other riders. Hands raised high, they embraced the exhilarating ups and downs of the ride, a metaphor for the journey they were on together.

The pirate ship ride was more than just an amusement park attraction for them; it was a celebration of their unity, their shared joy, and the collective courage to embrace life's highs and lows together. As the ship swayed and dipped, their laughter rang out, pure and unbridled, a testament to the happiness they found in each other's company. It was these moments, Ava realized, that painted the true picture of family - not just in the quiet, tender instances, but in the wild, joyous journey they were embarking on together.

The quiet of the evening enveloped them as they arrived home, the joyous echoes of the day still lingering in their hearts. Brian, ever the gentle presence, carefully carried a sleeping Lily into her room, his movements tender and full of love. As he tucked her in and planted a soft kiss on her forehead, Ava watched from the doorway, her heart brimming with gratitude for the beautiful day they had shared.

"She's completely out," Ava whispered with a soft laugh, carefully closing Lily's door behind them. Turning to Brian, her eyes shone with sincerity. "Thank you, Bri, for everything today. You've brought so much joy into our lives, especially Lily's."

Brian's response was a gentle touch, his hand caressing her face with a tenderness that spoke volumes. "Seeing you and Lily so happy, it means everything to me. I love you both so much, Ava," he confessed, his voice carrying the weight of his emotions.

Ava felt the warmth of his words settle in her heart, yet she found herself at a loss for words, unable to echo his sentiments. The conflict within her was palpable, and a part of her felt a twinge of guilt for not being able to reciprocate his feelings openly.

Sensing her struggle, Brian offered a soft, understanding chuckle. His eyes, filled with patience and empathy, met hers. "It's alright. You don't have to say anything. My love isn't conditional, Ava. I just want you to know, every day, how much I love you," he assured her, his hand lingering on her face, a silent promise in his touch.

As he turned to leave, Ava, moved by the day's events and Brian's unwavering affection, acted on an impulse. She stepped forward and lightly kissed his cheek, a small but significant gesture that took Brian by surprise.

"What was that for?" he asked, a grin spreading across his face, his surprise mingling with delight.

With a playful shrug, Ava's laughter filled the space between them. "Consider it a token of appreciation for today," she replied, her eyes twinkling with mirth. "Good night, Brian."

In that moment, as Brian stood at the threshold, a quiet understanding passed between them. His self-restraint was evident, a testament to his respect for her feelings and the pace at which she was comfortable moving forward. With a final smile and a nod, he stepped out into the night, leaving Ava with a heart full of gratitude, affection, and the gentlest flutter of something new beginning to stir within.

As Ava and Lily enjoyed their leisurely brunch, Ava decided it was the perfect time to share some exciting news. "Hey sweetie, guess what? Granddad and Grandmom are coming to visit in two days," she said, watching Lily's reaction closely.

Lily's face lit up instantly. "Yay! I missed them so much, mommy! Is Uncle Nate coming too?" she asked, her enthusiasm barely contained as she nibbled on her broccoli.

Ava felt a twinge of regret as she responded, "Uncle Nate's really busy and can't make it this time. But he's sending a big box of toys with your grandparents."

Lily's excitement dimmed slightly, but she quickly perked up again. Ava knew how much Lily adored her Uncle Nate, almost as much as she adored Brian. Speaking of Brian, Ava had something on her mind she wanted to discuss with Lily.

"Uh, sweetie... what do you think about Brian?" Ava ventured cautiously, her gaze flitting between her daughter and her plate.

Without hesitation, Lily's smile widened. "Daddy Brian is the best! He's always so nice and fun!"

Encouraged by Lily's response, Ava ventured further. "And how would you feel if he became mommy's boyfriend? Do you know what that means?"

Lily nodded, her expression turning surprisingly serious for a moment. "Does that mean he'll be around even more? Like a real daddy?"

Ava was taken aback by the directness of Lily's question. "Well, yes, something like that. But, sweetie, that's a big step. What would you think about that?"

But Lily's excitement was undeterred. "I want Daddy Brian to be my real daddy, Mommy. Please, please!" she pleaded, her enthusiasm bubbling over.

Ava laughed, both touched and slightly overwhelmed by Lily's enthusiasm. "Let's take it one step at a time, okay? But I'm really glad you like the idea," she said, her heart feeling lighter.

Just then, Ava noticed Lily's gaze drift towards the window, her little face lighting up. "Look, Mommy, Daddy Brian's back!" Lily exclaimed, hopping off her chair and rushing to the door.

Lily's enthusiasm was contagious, her excitement filling the room as she flung open the door to greet Brian. "Daddy Brian!"

she squealed, her joy uncontainable as she bounced on the spot.

"Hey there, Princess! Good morning!" Brian's voice was tender and full of affection as he scooped Lily into his arms. He shot a playful glance towards Ava, "Looks like someone's in high spirits today, huh?"

Lily, still in Brian's arms, beamed with innocent boldness. "Daddy Brian, are you gonna be my real daddy soon?"

Ava, caught off guard by Lily's direct question, felt her cheeks flush with embarrassment. "Lily!" she exclaimed, her tone a gentle chiding.

Brian's eyebrows rose in amused curiosity. "Have you two been talking about me before I came in?" he asked, his grin widening.

Ava, desperate to steer the conversation away from the topic, interjected quickly. "Lily, why don't you go back and finish cleaning up your toys like you promised, okay? We can talk about all this later," she said, her voice a blend of distraction and mild panic.

Lily, sensing the shift in mood, hesitated but then nodded obediently. "Okay, mommy," she said, giving Brian a quick hug before scampering off to her play area.

As Lily left the room, Ava exhaled a sigh of relief, her heart still racing from the unexpected turn the conversation had taken. She wasn't quite ready to share her thoughts with Brian, not without having the chance to dress up and mentally prepare for what felt like a significant step forward in their relationship.

Brian, sensing Ava's discomfort, decided not to press the topic further. "Kids, they say the darndest things, don't they?" he chuckled, trying to ease the tension.

Ava managed a small smile, grateful for Brian's understanding. "Yeah, they really do. Lily's got quite the imagination," she replied, her mind already racing ahead to how she would approach this conversation with Brian when the moment was right.

As Ava watched Brian interact with Lily, a sense of warmth and admiration filled her heart. She knew the decision she was leaning towards was a big one, and it deserved the right setting, the right moment. For now, she was content to let the morning unfold, knowing that the conversation about the future, about what Brian meant to her and Lily, would come in its own time, under the right circumstances.

With Lily happily preoccupied, Ava turned her attention back to Brian, her curiosity piqued. "So, what brings you by this morning? It's always a pleasure to see you, of course," she inquired, her tone light yet genuinely interested.

Brian set down a cup on the counter, the aroma of caramel and coffee filling the air. "I was in the neighborhood and thought you might enjoy this—your favorite, iced caramel latte," he said, his casual demeanor belying the thoughtfulness of the gesture. "And, well, there's another reason too. I wanted to ask if you'd join me for a proper date tonight, just the two of us. I think it's time we had a little grown-up time away from our usual routine."

Ava's heart skipped a beat at the invitation. The idea of spending an evening with Brian, away from the responsibilities of parenthood, was both exciting and nerve-wracking.

"Who will look after Lily?" she asked, the protective mother in her needing reassurance.

Brian smiled, understanding her concern. "My sister volunteered to babysit. She adores Lily, and I trust her completely. It'll just be for a few hours, and Lily will be in great hands," he assured her, his confidence soothing Ava's apprehension.

After a moment's reflection, Ava found herself nodding, a smile spreading across her face. "Okay, yes. Let's do it. A date sounds wonderful," she agreed, the prospect of spending quality time with Brian sparking a flutter of excitement in her.

Brian's eyes lit up at her response, a mixture of relief and happiness evident in his expression. "Fantastic! I'll pick you up at seven. Dress casually; I've got something laid-back in mind," he said, his tone laced with anticipation.

In the quiet of Lily's bedroom, the soft glow of the nightlight painted a serene scene as Ava tucked her daughter into bed. The usual bedtime routine was tinged with a touch of excitement tonight due to Ava's upcoming date with Brian. "Sweetie, Aunt Mary will be here soon to look after you while I go out with Brian for a little while, okay? Make sure you're on your best behavior. I won't be gone long," Ava reassured Lily, her voice soft and comforting.

Lily, tucked snugly under her blankets, nodded with understanding. "I will, Mommy. Don't worry," she replied, her voice sleepy but content. However, the stillness of the moment was pierced by Lily's sudden, thoughtful question. "Mommy, does daddy love me?" she asked, her small voice filled with innocent curiosity.

The question caught Ava off guard, a gentle reminder of conversations she knew they would eventually have to face. She sat down at the edge of Lily's bed, her hand tenderly pushing back a curl from her daughter's forehead. "Your Daddy Brian? Yes, he does, baby," Ava replied softly, her heart tugging with a mix of emotions. Ava reassured her.

Lily, her understanding beyond her years, shook her head slightly. "No, Mommy. I mean my real dad," she clarified.

Ava drew in a breath, steadying herself for the delicate conversation. "Yes, sweetie, he does. He loves you very much, even though he hasn't had the chance to meet you yet. Do you want to know a little secret?" Ava ventured, her voice a soothing melody in the dimly lit room.

Lily's eyes widened with the promise of a secret. "Yes, mommy! Please tell me!"

Ava smiled, the warmth in her heart pushing through the complexity of her emotions. "Well, your daddy is the one who picked your name, Lily. He loved lilies – they were his favorite flowers. He always said that lilies are elegant and beautiful, just like he imagined his daughter would be. And you know what? He was absolutely right."

Lily's face lit up with a delighted smile, her imagination ignited by the story of her name. Ava's heart swelled with love for her daughter, and despite the complexity of her feelings about Ethan, she was determined to keep the memory of him positive for Lily.

"Now, it's time to sleep, my little Lily," Ava said, tucking the covers snugly around her daughter.

"Goodnight, mommy. I love you," Lily murmured, her eyelids fluttering closed.

"Goodnight, my darling. I love you more," Ava whispered, watching her daughter drift into sleep, a peaceful expression on her face. Turning off the light, Ava left the room with a bittersweet feeling in her heart. She knew that one day she would have to explain more about Ethan to Lily, but for now, she was content to let her daughter cherish the beautiful image of a father who loved her, even from afar.

As Ava sat in the quiet of her living room, the gentle rhythm of anticipation for the evening with Brian was suddenly shattered by the piercing ring of her phone. It was Nate. With a light chuckle, Ava answered, "Hi Nate. Were you hoping to chat with Lily? She's just drifted off to sleep."

But the gravity in Nate's voice immediately pulled Ava into a sea of unease. "Sis..." His tone was laden with a weight that made Ava's heart sink.

"Nate, what's wrong? You're scaring me," Ava's voice trembled, each word heavy with worry.

Nate's sigh was like a harbinger of bad news, resonating through the phone with a deep, somber echo. "You need to come home, Ava. It's Dad. He... he had a heart attack during the press conference."

A cold shiver ran down Ava's spine. The press conference – her father's passionate project to bring medical care to the underprivileged – had been his dream. But now, it seemed, that dream had taken a grave toll.

"Daddy..." The word barely escaped Ava's lips, her voice a fragile whisper, as if speaking louder might confirm the harsh reality. Her father, her rock, the man whose compassion and dedication had inspired so many, lay vulnerable and fighting for his life.

Panic and resolve clashed within her. "I'm on my way, Nate. Tell me everything when I get there," she said, a surge of determination steadying her trembling voice.

The knock at the door arrived at a world that had shifted on its axis. It was Brian and Mary. The moment Ava's eyes met Brian's, the floodgates opened. Tears streamed down her face, each one a testament to the fear, love, and turmoil that coursed through her.

"Ava, tell me what's happened," Brian urged, his voice a blend of concern and a deep desire to provide comfort.

Through her sobs, Ava relayed the devastating news. "It's my father, Brian. He had a heart attack. He's in the hospital, and I... I have to go to New York immediately."

The shock was palpable on both Brian and Mary's faces. But in the midst of the whirlwind, Brian's resolve was unshakeable. "I'm with you, Ava. We'll go to the airport now," he said, his voice firm, leaving no room for debate.

With swift, efficient movements, Brian made his way to Lily's room, while Ava, her hands shaking, attempted to pack what

THE ILLUSION OF US

they needed. Lily, still half-asleep but sensing the urgency in the air, nodded and allowed Brian to help her get ready. Ava, meanwhile, was a flurry of action, packing essentials and trying to mentally prepare for the emotional journey back to New York.

Brian reappeared, Lily now fully awake and clinging to him. "Ava, everything's set. I've called the airport; we'll have a flight within the next two hours," he informed her, his voice steady but his concern for Ava clearly etched on his face.

Ava, her suitcase in hand, took a deep breath and looked at Brian, her eyes brimming with tears but also gratitude. "Brian, I... thank you. I don't know how to thank you enough."

Brian gently placed his hand on her shoulder, offering a reassuring squeeze. "No thanks needed. Let's just get you to your dad. That's all that matters right now."

The life she had carefully built in the quiet comfort of Ketchikan was calling her back to the bustling, complicated streets of New York – back to a past that she had left behind but that now needed her more than ever.

CHAPTER SEVENTEEN

As they sat in the car, the quiet hum of the engine a stark contrast to the storm of emotions within, Ava felt a wave of apprehension wash over her. The decision to keep Lily away from the hospital's potentially distressing environment weighed heavily on her, yet she knew it was the right choice given the uncertainty of her father's condition. Brian's presence beside her, steady and reassuring, was the only solace in the midst of her swirling thoughts.

"Bri, I can't tell you how much it means to have you here," Ava said, her voice quivering slightly as she glanced his way. The gratitude in her eyes was clear, even as they glistened with unshed tears.

Brian navigated the car through the streets with a calmness that seemed to defy the gravity of the situation. Turning to Ava, he offered her a warm, reassuring smile. "Ava, you don't have to thank me. I'm here for you, for Lily, for whatever you need. Just knowing I can be here to support you during this time is all that matters," he said, his hand finding hers, giving it a gentle, supportive squeeze.

In the dim light of the car's interior, the bond between Ava and Brian was a silent testament to the strength and comfort that comes from shared burdens and unwavering companionship. As they drove towards the hospital, the road ahead uncertain, it was the certainty of their connection that fortified Ava, giving her the courage to face the challenges that lay ahead. As they approached the medical center, Ava turned to Lily. "Baby, I'll come get you later, okay? Be a good girl for me, won't you, my little Lily?" she said lovingly.

Lily nodded, her childish innocence shining through. "I promise, Mommy."

Ava kissed her forehead, relieved by her daughter's easygoing nature.

Brian, seeing Ava's concern, tried to lighten the mood. "Lily, Daddy Brian is going to take you somewhere fun. Ready?"

Lily's grin lit up her face. "Yay! Bye, Mommy!"

Ava waved them off before entering the hospital, her heart pounding with anxiety. She was anxious, not just about her father's condition but also the possibility of encountering Ethan. She hadn't prepared herself for that yet.

At the nurse's station, Ava was greeted with surprised but warm welcomes. "Miss Greenwood, welcome back," said Nurse Susan. Ava asked for her father's room and was led to the VIP wing.

As the door to her father's hospital room swung open, Ava's heart leapt into her throat. Standing there, her family's expressions transformed from shock to unbridled joy. "Dad!" she cried out, her voice choked with emotion as she rushed to the bedside. She threw her arms around her father, holding him tightly as tears cascaded down her cheeks.

"Oh, Daddy, please tell me you're okay," she sobbed, her body trembling with the intensity of the moment.

Her father, weak but smiling, wrapped his arms around her. "I'm much better now, princess," he said, his voice a comforting balm. "Seeing you, right here, is the best medicine I could ever ask for."

As Ava turned from her father's bedside to face her mother and Nate, the raw emotion in their eyes mirrored her own. She stepped closer to her mother, wrapping her arms around her in a tight embrace. "Oh, Mommy, this must have been so hard for you," she whispered, her voice quivering as she felt her mother's body tremble with silent sobs.

Her mother clung to her, the years of worry and care flowing out in her tears. "Ava, it's such a relief to have you here. And you need to tell your father to slow down. It seems he only listens to you these days," she said, her voice a mixture of relief and lingering fear.

Nate, ever the protective older brother, moved closer, his presence a comforting constant. "Hey, little sis, where's my favorite niece? Lily must be wondering about all this fuss," he asked, trying to lighten the mood.

Ava managed a small smile, appreciating Nate's attempt to inject some normalcy into the tense atmosphere. "She's with Brian for now. I'll bring her by the house later, don't worry."

Nate's eyebrows raised inquisitively, a hint of a smirk playing at the corner of his mouth. "Oh, so Brian's here too, huh? How are things going there? Any news you want to share with your favorite brother?" he teased, his tone light but curious.

Ava playfully nudged him, her heart momentarily lighter amidst the worry. "Nate, not now. But trust me, you'll be the first to know when there's something to tell," she promised, grateful for the brief respite from the heavy emotions of the day.

Nate chuckled, not deterred by her response. "Come on, Ava, you've got to give me something. I've been waiting five years for some action in this storyline. It's like my own personal telenovela," he joked, his humor a welcome distraction.

Their parents, witnessing the exchange, allowed themselves a momentary respite from their worries, finding a small measure of peace in the playful interaction between their children.

The door opened again, introducing a new wave of tension. "Ava..." The voice was familiar, achingly so.

There, in the doorway, stood Ethan. His face was a complex tapestry of shock, regret, and something that looked painfully like love. Their eyes met, and for a moment, the world seemed to fall away, leaving only the two of them in the silent echo of their shared past.

The room was heavy with emotion, charged with the unspoken words and feelings that lingered in the air. Ava stood frozen, caught between the family she had just embraced and the man who had once meant everything to her.

Ethan stood there, just as striking as she remembered, his doctor's white coat doing little to mask the charisma that had always been a part of him. Five years seemed to have merely polished the Ethan she once knew, his presence as captivating as ever.

Ava felt a tumult of emotions as she stood there, her heart racing inexplicably. She couldn't understand why the sight of him was stirring feelings she believed were long gone. She had spent years rebuilding her life, finding peace and a new direction, and yet, here she was, her pulse quickening, her mind reeling at the sight of Ethan.

Silently, she scolded herself, frustrated at her own reaction. 'This isn't me anymore,' she thought, trying to steady her racing heart. 'I've moved on.' But the flutter in her chest told a different story, a reminder of a past that wasn't as distant as she'd convinced herself it was.

In the hospital room, Ethan was forced to maintain a strictly professional demeanor, owing to his role as Mr. Greenwood's attending doctor. Surrounded by his team of nurses and resident doctors, he had to navigate the delicate balance of addressing his patient's health concerns while also contending with the unexpected presence of Ava.

"Mr. Greenwood, you've suffered a mild heart attack," Ethan began, his voice steady and clinical. He carefully explained the situation, conscious of the watchful eyes of his medical team. "The primary cause appears to be stress, likely from overworking. It's critical that you take a step back and focus on your recovery."

As Ethan spoke, his gaze involuntarily shifted to Ava, causing a momentary flicker in his otherwise composed expression. Ava, acutely aware of his glances, felt a wave of emotions but remained silent, trying to process the flood of memories Ethan's presence brought.

Ethan continued, outlining the medical advice and precautions. "Rest is essential, and reducing work-related stress is crucial to prevent any further incidents. We need to ensure there isn't a recurrence."

Nate, sensing the underlying tension, interjected with words of thanks. "Thank you, Ethan. It's reassuring to know our father is in capable hands."

Ethan nodded, acknowledging the gratitude. "Of course. It's important that Mr. Greenwood follows these guidelines. My team and I are available should you need any further assistance."

As Ethan wrapped up his medical briefing, he made a move to leave the room. Just before exiting, he paused, his eyes instinctively seeking out Ava. Their gazes met, holding a moment that seemed to stretch beyond time. In Ethan's eyes, there was a clear yearning to say something, a multitude of unspoken words hanging between them.

The room, already heavy with the emotional weight of Ava's unexpected return and Mr. Greenwood's health concerns, grew even more charged in that silent exchange. Ava, caught in Ethan's gaze, felt a familiar tug in her heart, a reminder of all they had once been to each other.

Ethan's mouth opened slightly, as if he was about to speak, but then he seemed to reconsider. Whatever he wanted to say remained unvoiced, lost in the complexity of their shared past and the current situation. The tension in his expression was evident, reflecting his internal struggle between professional responsibilities and personal emotions.

Finally, with a subtle shake of his head as if to clear his thoughts, Ethan turned away, breaking the connection. He stepped out of the room, leaving Ava and her family behind. His departure was quiet but filled with a sense of unresolved matters, leaving Ava with a mixture of relief and a deep, aching sense of longing.

As the door closed behind Ethan, Ava let out a quiet breath she hadn't realized she was holding. Ava's mind was still reeling from the encounter. Ethan's brief glance had reopened old wounds, reminding her of a chapter in her life she had thought was closed.

In the hospital room, after Ethan's departure, Nate looked at Ava, sensing the emotional turmoil that his sister was going through. Trying to lighten the mood but also address the elephant in the room, he asked gently, "So, how is it seeing Ethan after all these years?" His voice carried a teasing edge, but his eyes were full of concern for his sister.

Ava turned to face him, her emotional defenses crumbling. Her eyes quickly filled with tears, and she raised her hand in a vain attempt to fan them away. With a voice choked with emotion, she managed to say, "I... I thought I was okay..." Her words were punctuated by a sob and a strained, painful laugh, revealing the depth of her unresolved feelings for Ethan.

Seeing her distress, her mother immediately wrapped Ava in a comforting embrace. Ava leaned into her mother's arms, surrendering to the wave of emotions she had been holding back. She cried openly, her tears flowing freely, each one speaking to the enduring pain and love she still felt for Ethan.

Her mother held her close, murmuring words of comfort, while Nate watched on, his face a mix of sympathy and protectiveness.

Ethan, determined to have a moment with Ava after his surgery, hurried back to Mr. Greenwood's room. As he approached the VIP left wing in the late afternoon, his heart raced with anticipation, hoping that Ava was still there.

However, as he turned the corner, he saw Ava walking away. He called out her name, but his voice was lost in the bustling noise of the hospital. Quickening his pace, Ethan followed her through the corridors, his anxiety mounting with each step.

As he reached the parking lot, his eyes locked onto a scene that stopped him in his tracks. There was Ava, with a man he didn't recognize, who was holding a little girl in his arms. Ethan watched, his heart sinking, as Ava bent down to kiss the child lovingly.

"Mommy, Daddy Brian took me to the zoo and I saw lots and lots of animals. They were so cute!" the little girl exclaimed with innocent joy.

Ethan stood frozen, the realization hitting him like a tidal wave. Ava had a child and, by all appearances, had moved on with her life, seemingly married to this 'Daddy Brian.' A myriad of emotions coursed through him—surprise, pain, and a deep sense of loss.

As Ava and the man, presumably Brian, walked towards their car with the child, Ethan remained rooted to the spot, struggling to process the scene before him. The sight of Ava as a mother, the happiness in her voice, and her apparent new life – it all seemed surreal.

Ethan's world, once anchored by the hope of rekindling something with Ava, now felt unmoored. The weight of his missed opportunities and the choices he had made settled heavily upon him. As Ava and her family drove away, Ethan was left to confront the harsh reality of his situation, grappling with the profound impact of seeing Ava, not just as the woman he once loved, but as a mother and partner to someone else.

Devastated by the revelation in the hospital parking lot, Ethan sought refuge in the familiar dim lights of a local bar. He wasn't ready to face the pain of seeing Ava with another man and a child, so his goal for the night was simple: to drown his sorrows in alcohol.

As he nursed his whisky, lost in a tumult of emotions, the door swung open, and in walked Tony, Ethan's best friend. Tony had received a call from Ethan earlier, telling him his whereabouts. He took a seat next to Ethan, ordering a gin and tonic with a casual ease.

"You look like it's the end of the world, man. What's the matter?" Tony tried to inject some lightness into the situation with a chuckle.

Ethan, however, was in no mood for banter. He downed the remaining whisky in his glass and signaled for another, ignoring Tony's attempt at conversation.

"Hey Ethan, you trying to get drunk tonight?" Tony asked, his tone shifting to concern. "The last time I saw you like this was when Ava left..."

At the mention of Ava's name, Ethan turned sharply towards Tony, a storm brewing in his eyes. "Ava's back," he revealed bluntly.

Tony's reaction was one of shock. "What? When? Did you guys talk? Are you getting back together?" His questions came rapid-fire, a mix of hope and surprise.

Ethan let out a heavy sigh, his frustration evident. "Would I be here like this if we were?" he snapped back, his voice laced with bitterness.

Tony tried to lighten the mood, but his chuckle felt out of place. "Chill, man. What happened then?"

Ethan took another sip of his whisky, the burn of the alcohol a temporary distraction from his emotional pain. "She's married... and she has a kid now. Ava has moved on. And I'm just wasted," he confessed, his voice hollow.

Tony exhaled deeply, his mind reeling from the news. He remembered all too well the state Ethan was in when Ava left. He had been a wreck, seeking solace in alcohol and endless searches for her. Now, Tony feared for his friend's well-being, knowing how much Ava's return and the revelation of her new life would impact him.

Reaching out, Tony placed a comforting hand on Ethan's shoulder. It was a gesture of silent support, an acknowledgment of the pain his friend was going through. In that crowded bar, amidst the clinking glasses and murmured conversations, two friends sat together, one trying to escape his heartache, the other offering a steady presence in the midst of a storm.

Tony, seeing Ethan in no state to drive, took on the role of the responsible friend and drove him home. Tony lingered in his car, watching until Ethan made it safely through the gate of the apartment complex. He wanted to make sure his friend was okay before driving away. He finally pulled away, his mind still heavy with concern for Ethan's well-being.

Ethan took a deep, steadying breath before opening the front door. Stepping into the apartment felt like walking into a world of memories, each one echoing Ava's absence. Despite the pain it brought him, Ethan couldn't bring himself to leave this place, their shared sanctuary where every corner held traces of their life together.

Stumbling through the living room, Ethan made his way to the bedroom, each step feeling heavier than the last. He let his body fall onto the bed, the familiar sheets offering no comfort. Reaching out with unsteady hands, he picked up a picture frame from the nightstand. It was a photo of him and Ava, smiling, captured in a moment of unguarded happiness.

As a solitary tear traced its path down Ethan's cheek, he gazed longingly at Ava's image in the photo frame. Holding it close, he whispered hoarsely, "I missed you so much, babe..." Each word was laden with a deep, raw emotion, revealing the turmoil within him. His heart ached intensely, an agonizing tightness that made it difficult to draw breath.

He continued, his voice barely above a whisper, filled with longing and despair. "I'm lost without you, Ava. Knowing you're married now... it's like I've lost my anchor. Loving you was the one thing that kept me grounded, that gave me purpose."

Ethan's voice broke as he struggled to articulate the depth of his feelings. "What am I supposed to do now, Ava? How do I keep going, knowing you've moved on?" His plea was heartfelt, a desperate search for guidance in his sea of sorrow.

Tears streamed down his face, each one silently bearing witness to the profound love and loss he felt. "I need you, baby.

Please, just tell me what to do," he murmured to the photograph, aching for an answer he knew wouldn't come.

In that moment, alone with his memories and the ghost of a love that once filled his life, Ethan felt lost, adrift in a sea of sorrow. The revelation of Ava's new life had shattered the fragile hope he held onto, leaving him to confront a future without her. His sobs filled the quiet room, the sound of a heart breaking all over again.

In the tranquil ambiance of the Greenwood residence, with the gentle laughter of Lily and her grandparents echoing through the grand hall, Ava sat lost in her thoughts. Her brother Nate, ever perceptive, noticed her distant gaze and decided it was time for a heart-to-heart.

"What's on your mind, little sis?" he asked, his voice gentle yet probing.

Ava offered a wan smile. "Just a few things that keep bothering me," she replied, her voice a soft murmur.

Nate leaned forward, his eyes locking with hers. "Let me take a wild guess. Ethan's on your mind, isn't he?" he said, a knowing smile on his lips.

Ava let out a soft chuckle, tinged with a hint of pain. "Am I that transparent? It's ridiculous, right? After all this time, after

I've healed and moved on, just seeing him there... it rattled me, Nate."

Nate nodded, his expression understanding. "Ava, you two have a history. It's not just about throwing away feelings or memories; it's about acknowledging them. They were a part of your life."

Ava's response was a scoff. "You mean those 'fake' feelings, right?" Her words were heavy, laden with past hurt.

"Do you honestly believe they were all fake?" Nate asked, his gaze steady and unwavering.

"Well, he made it quite clear, didn't he?" Ava shrugged, her defenses rising. "But I'm done dwelling on the past, Nate. I spent enough time doing that. I want to focus on being happy now."

Nate's smile was warm, supportive. "And you think Brian is the key to that happiness?"

There was a shy nod from Ava. "I do. In fact, I was about to tell him that I'm ready to start dating him right before you called that night."

"So, what's holding you back? Dad's on the mend, you're free to make your own choices. Why not reach out to Brian?" Nate's question was gentle but pointed.

THE ILLUSION OF US

Ava's silence spoke volumes. She knew her brother's question was simple, yet she found herself without an answer. Her mind wandered back to the unexpected encounter with Ethan, the way her emotions had surged unbidden.

A silence fell, heavy with unspoken thoughts. Ava's mind raced, unable to pinpoint why she hadn't reached out to Brian yet. Was it really just the busyness of caring for her father, or was there something more, something deeper holding her back?

Nate's voice, light but incisive, broke the quiet. "Meeting Ethan again threw you off balance, didn't it? Made you second-guess your feelings?"

Ava shot him a glare, frustration mingling with admiration at how well her brother could read her. "Nate, just say what you want to say. Are you suggesting that deep down, I might still want to be with Ethan?"

Nate held her gaze, his expression serious yet open. "I'm not suggesting anything, Ava. I just want you to be honest with yourself. What is it that you truly want?"

Ava hesitated, her words a whisper more to herself than to Nate. "I... no, of course not. I don't want to go back to that." But even as she spoke, Ava felt a stirring of doubt, a whisper of what-ifs that refused to be silenced.

Their heartfelt conversation was paused as their parents and Lily joined them, laughter and joy filling the air. Ava quickly composed herself, holding Lily close and showering her with kisses, masking the turmoil inside her.

Their father's voice was filled with a newfound energy as he addressed the room. "I've been thinking, now that Ava is back and we have a new member in the family," he began, his eyes twinkling with excitement, "why don't we throw a grand Christmas celebration next week? It's a perfect occasion to introduce Lily to everyone."

Ava's heart skipped a beat at his words. The thought of such a public introduction of Lily, especially with the likelihood of Ethan and his family being invited, sent a wave of anxiety through her. She opened her mouth, intending to express her concerns, "But Dad..."

However, she caught herself, seeing the sheer joy and anticipation in her father's eyes. He had always loved grand gestures, and this was his way of embracing a joyous family reunion after his recent health scare.

Nate, ever the supportive brother, immediately chimed in, "Let's do it, Dad. It'll be wonderful."

Her mother turned towards Ava, her expression a mixture of excitement and inquiry. "Ava, darling, what do you think?"

Ava hesitated, torn between her own trepidation and the desire to make her family happy. With a deep breath, she mustered a smile. "Sure, if it makes you happy, let's have the party," she said, her voice laced with a quiet resolve.

Her agreement set into motion the plans for a festive gathering. But as she watched her family buzz with excitement, Ava's thoughts were elsewhere. The Christmas party would not only be a celebration but also a moment of truth. When Ethan learns of Lily's existence, it would change everything. She wasn't sure if she was ready for that confrontation, but now she had no choice. The approaching party hung over her like a promise of inevitable change, leaving her heart heavy with both anticipation and apprehension.

The Greenwood Mansion was abuzz with festive energy on the night of the grand Christmas party. Despite the last-minute nature of the event, the vast halls of the mansion were filled with guests, a testament to the Greenwoods' standing in the community. The mansion was a winter wonderland, adorned with twinkling lights, elegant garlands, and a towering Christmas tree that sparkled with ornaments and shimmering tinsel. The air was filled with the sound of laughter, music, and the clinking of glasses, creating a joyful ambiance that encapsulated the spirit of the season.

Ava, the star of the evening, was a vision in a stunning red dress that hugged her curves elegantly. The dress was both sophisticated and festive, with a neckline that enhanced her natural grace and a hem that swayed with her every movement.

THE ILLUSION OF US

Her hair was styled in loose waves, framing her face and highlighting her radiant smile. She moved through the crowd with ease, her presence drawing admiring glances from the guests.

As she assisted her parents and Nate in welcoming the attendees, Ava felt a mix of excitement and nervousness. She was acutely aware that Ethan might appear at any moment, but as the evening progressed, there was no sign of him. She couldn't decide if she was relieved or disappointed.

As Ava mingled among the guests, she felt a tap on her shoulder. Turning around, she found herself face-to-face with Ethan's parents. Their smiles were warm and genuine, bringing a mix of nostalgia and apprehension to her heart.

"Mr. and Mrs. Williams, it's so good to see you," Ava greeted them, her voice carrying a hint of surprise.

"Ava dear, you look absolutely stunning," Ethan's mother complimented, her eyes taking in Ava's elegant attire. "We were so thrilled to hear you've returned. How have you been?"

Ava felt a rush of emotions but managed a smile. "Thank you, Mrs. Williams. I've been well, finding my way, you could say."

Ethan's father joined in, his voice tinged with a fatherly concern. "We've missed seeing you around, Ava. Ethan hasn't been the same since you left."

Ava's heart skipped a beat at the mention of Ethan, but she maintained her composure. "Ethan's a strong person. I'm sure he's doing just fine," she replied, trying to sound casual.

His mother nodded, a soft sigh escaping her lips. "Yes, he is strong. But it's clear he misses you. He's never really talked about it, but we can tell."

Ethan's father smiled. "You always had a special bond, both of you. It was something quite remarkable to witness."

As the party continued, Ava found herself occasionally glancing towards the entrance, her heart skipping a beat each time the door opened. Part of her hoped to see Ethan walk through those doors, while another part feared the confrontation that would inevitably follow.

Tired from the evening's social engagements, Ava sought solace on the other side of the expansive mansion, far from the bustling crowd. With a wine glass cradled in her hand, she stepped out onto the terrace, where the winter breeze caressed her skin, prompting her to wrap her arms around herself. Despite the chill, a wave of tranquility washed over her. She took a sip of her wine, each breath laden with unspoken yearnings.

Suddenly, a familiar voice, deep and resonant, stirred the air. "Hi..." It electrified Ava, sending shivers down her spine. As she turned, she saw Ethan, resplendent in a black lapel tuxedo, leaning nonchalantly against the wall. His intense gaze seemed to set her very soul ablaze. As always, he exuded an effortless charm, his smile captivating.

"H...Hi Ethan," Ava stammered, her voice quivering. "I thought you weren't coming." Her words, unintentionally tinged with sadness, betrayed her feelings.

Ethan's smile grew lopsided, revealing his charming dimple. "If I didn't know better, I'd think you were disappointed thinking I wasn't here tonight," he teased, his voice warm yet playful.

"What are you doing here, Ethan?" Ava managed to ask, her nerves tingling in his presence.

Ethan approached her slowly, a glass of gin and tonic in hand. "I was invited," he chuckled, a sound that made Ava's heart skip a beat. "I also came because I wanted to see you."

Ava felt a blush creep up her cheeks under Ethan's intense gaze. His presence still affected her deeply. Subconsciously, she touched her cheek, trying to hide her flush.

"You're still the same, Ava. I can still make you blush with such ease." His smile turned bittersweet as he sipped his drink. "Where have you been these past five years? Did you know I've looked for you everywhere? Were you so angry with me that you hid yourself all this time?"

THE ILLUSION OF US

Their eyes locked, with Ava looking away first. "Ethan, it's all in the past. I've forgotten it," she said, trying to sound strong, unaffected.

Ethan nodded, a look of hurt flashing across his face. "I know. You moved on, built a life... a family of your own."

Confusion furrowed Ava's brow. "What are you talking about, Ethan?"

"Last week, I saw you with your husband and daughter at the hospital parking lot. She's adorable, looks just like you. And your husband, quite the handsome man," he said, his voice laced with pain and regret.

Ava recalled the day Brian picked her up from the hospital. "You mean Brian?"

"Yeah, I heard your daughter call him 'Daddy Brian'," Ethan replied, his jealousy apparent.

Ava hesitated, her heart pounding, knowing full well that Brian wasn't her husband. Yet, in that moment, under Ethan's intense gaze, she chose her words carefully. "Yeah, you could say that," she replied, her voice steady but her mind racing with the implications of her answer.

In the quiet room, the tension was palpable. Ava's heart raced, torn between a past she thought she had moved on from and the present she had painstakingly built. Ethan's proximity, his familiar scent, and the soft caress on her cheek threatened to unravel her resolve. His words, heavy with regret and longing, hit her like a tidal wave.

"I've missed you, baby... Please tell me you've missed me too," Ethan implored, his eyes a mirror of vulnerability and desperation.

Ava's instinct was to recoil, to put distance between them, but Ethan's presence was overwhelming, his hands on the wall caging her in. "Ethan, let me go. Are you drunk or something?" she demanded, her voice a mix of frustration and fear.

Ethan's intensity didn't waver. "If I were drunk, Ava, I would've kissed you by now. But I'm holding back, can't you see? I'm trying so hard not to pull you into my arms."

His raw honesty, the confession of his restraint, only deepened the turmoil within Ava. "Why are you doing this, Ethan? I let you go, so you could be happy. Why can't you let me do the same?"

As she attempted to escape, Ethan's grip on her hand tightened. His sigh was heavy, laden with a remorse that seemed to saturate the very air. "I'm sorry, Ava. Only after you left did I realize the enormity of my mistakes. Life without you... it's been an endless struggle, a mess of regrets."

His words igniting a flicker of the old flame she thought had extinguished long ago. But she steeled herself, pushing against the flood of memories and what-ifs.

Ethan's words hung heavy in the air, a confession that sent ripples through the stillness of the room. "I want you back, Ava..." he uttered, the intensity of his longing palpable. Ava's breath hitched, her body tensing as Ethan pulled her into an unexpected embrace from behind. "I know it's foolish to hope, especially now that you have a family of your own. But seeing you again, all I want is to hold you close, to have a chance to make you love me again," he whispered, his voice a mix of desperation and sincerity.

Ava's heart wavered, caught in a tempest of past affections and present realities. Ethan's embrace, once her sanctuary, now felt like a storm she wasn't sure she could weather. His words, steeped in regret and yearning, stirred a tumult of emotions within her. She felt the old scars of their shared history pulsate, a reminder of the love that had once defined her world. And yet, there was a part of her that recoiled, a voice whispering caution, reminding her of the pain and betrayal that had once torn her world apart.

The conflict was written all over her face—a blend of pain, longing, and an undeniable fear of giving in to a past that had left deep marks on her soul. Ethan's touch, his proximity, was both a comfort and a torment, awakening memories and feelings she thought she had sealed away.

Gathering her resolve, Ava slowly disentangled herself from Ethan's embrace. "Our story had ended a long time ago, Ethan. I've accepted it. You should do the same," she said, her voice a testament to the strength she had forged in the face of past heartbreaks.

The sudden entrance of Brian with Lily in his arms was like a lifeline, pulling Ava back from the brink. Brian's gaze met hers, a silent understanding passing between them, a recognition of the storm of emotions that had just raged through her. "Hey honey. Our princess is looking for you,"

Ava reached for Lily, her daughter's presence a grounding force. Lily's innocent question, "Who is he, Mommy?" echoed in the room, a stark reminder of the separate worlds that Ava now navigated.

Ava exchanged a glance with Brian, a silent communication passing between them. "He's just a friend, sweetie. Let's go back to the party," she said, her voice steady, her decision resolute.

As they left the room, Ethan remained, a solitary figure grappling with the reality of his choices. The sight of Ava with her new life, the family she had built away from him, was a bitter revelation. He was left to confront the enormity of his loss, the love that, despite his hopes and pleas, seemed to have slipped irrevocably through his fingers. In that moment, the weight of his longing and the sting of rejection were tangible—a silent plea for a second chance that hung unanswered in the air.

CHAPTER EIGHTEEN

In the quiet sanctuary of Ava's room, the festive sounds of the Christmas party seemed a world away. The room was dimly lit, casting soft shadows that mirrored the turmoil in Ava's heart. Brian stood by, his presence a silent support, as Ava grappled with the storm of emotions that Ethan's unexpected reappearance had unleashed.

Tears streamed down Ava's cheeks, each drop a testament to the inner conflict that tore at her. "Brian, I'm so sorry," she sobbed, her voice choked with emotion. "I thought I was ready. I thought my feelings for Ethan were long gone. I was about to tell you... to tell you that I was ready to be with you, to start a new chapter."

Brian listened, his expression a blend of compassion and pain. He had sensed the depth of Ava's turmoil but hearing the words spoken aloud brought a sharp sting of reality.

"But seeing Ethan again... it's like a floodgate has opened. I'm so confused, Brian. I never meant to lead you on, to give you hope only to... to take it back," Ava continued, her sobs punctuating the heavy silence.

Brian moved closer, his demeanor calm yet filled with an undeniable hurt. "Ava, do you want to go back to Ethan? Now that you know he still has feelings for you?" he asked, his voice steady but laden with the weight of the moment.

Ava shook her head, her tears not relenting. "No, it's not that simple. Yes, I still love him. I'd be lying if I said otherwise. But the hurt, the betrayal... I'm not ready to just forgive and forget. My heart... it's still healing, Brian. And now, it's just... it's just shattered."

In the quiet of the room, Ava's admission hung heavy. The revelation of her lingering love for Ethan, juxtaposed with her inability to forgive, painted a vivid picture of her inner conflict. Brian, his own heart aching, struggled to find the right words, to offer comfort without overstepping the boundaries of her turmoil.

"Ava, I won't pretend this doesn't hurt. But more than that, I care about you. I care about your happiness," Brian said, his voice a soft but firm anchor in the emotional storm. "You don't have to make any decisions right now. Just... just know that I'm here for you, regardless of what the future holds."

Ava looked up at Brian, her eyes reflecting a mix of gratitude and sorrow. "Thank you, Brian. For being so understanding, so patient. I'm just so sorry for all this... for everything."

The room, filled with the sound of Ava's quiet sobs and the unspoken words that lingered in the air, became a silent witness to the complexity of the human heart. In that moment, Brian and Ava, each grappling with their own pain and confusion, found a fragile solace in the shared understanding that sometimes, love and forgiveness are journeys that take more than just the willingness to move forward—they require the courage to navigate the intricate pathways of the heart.

In the dimly lit outdoor bar, the clink of glasses and the low murmur of distant conversations provided a backdrop to the solitary figure of Ethan, nursing his whiskey with a somber air. Nate spotted him from across the space, his brooding presence unmistakable. With a measured stride, Nate approached and took a seat beside him, noting the heavy shadows of despair etched on Ethan's face.

"What's got you looking like the world's about to end, Ethan?" Nate asked, his voice casual but observant.

Ethan exhaled deeply, his gaze fixed on the amber liquid swirling in his glass. "It's Ava. She's back, Nate. But she's... she's married," he confessed, the words heavy with regret and a pain that seemed to pierce through his stoic facade.

Nate couldn't help but let out a chuckle, the irony of the situation too stark to ignore. Ethan's expression darkened, a flicker of anger passing through his eyes, but he restrained himself, mindful of Nate's position as his boss and friend.

"This isn't a laughing matter, Nate. You know how long I've waited for Ava, how much I've hoped for a chance to make things right. And now, to find out she's married..." Ethan's voice trailed off, the ache in his heart finding solace only in the numbing embrace of the whiskey.

Nate clapped Ethan on the shoulder, his grin unwavering despite the gravity of his friend's plight. "She really told you she's married?" he prodded, his curiosity piqued.

Ethan nodded, his expression a complex tapestry of confusion and hurt. "I know I don't deserve an easy forgiveness, not after everything. But to think she's moved on, that she's married... It's like the ground's been pulled from under me," he admitted, his voice barely above a whisper.

Nate's expression softened, the seriousness of the moment tempering his initial amusement. "Ethan, you did hurt my sister deeply. I'd be lying if I said I wasn't tempted to give you a piece of my mind back then. But you're here now, bearing the consequences of your actions."

Ethan looked up, his eyes clouded with a mix of defiance and desolation. "Go ahead then, punch me if that's what you want. Maybe it'll hurt less than knowing I've lost Ava for good."

Nate sighed, the laughter fading from his lips as he leaned in closer, his voice dropping to a serious tone. "Ethan, my sister isn't married. Ava's not wearing anyone's ring but her own."

The revelation hit Ethan like a thunderbolt, his heart lurching in his chest, disbelief and relief warring for dominance. "She's not... What? Why would she..."

Nate raised his glass, a knowing glint in his eyes. "Maybe it's her way of testing the waters, seeing if you're serious about turning over a new leaf. Or maybe she's just not ready to face what's between you two. Either way, I think it's high time you sorted things out, don't you?"

Ethan sat back, the weight of the world momentarily lifted from his shoulders, replaced by a flicker of hope, a chance at redemption he thought he'd lost. "Merry Christmas, Ethan. Looks like this holiday just got a whole lot more interesting for you."

Ethan's newfound glimmer of hope was quickly clouded by a troubling thought. "But her daughter... she called that man 'Daddy Brian.' What's that about?" he questioned, the confusion evident in his furrowed brows.

Nate's laughter broke through the heavy air, lightening the mood. "Oh, you met Lily, huh? Isn't she just the cutest?" His fondness for his niece was unmistakable, a proud uncle through and through.

At the mention of the little girl's name, Ethan's world shifted on its axis. Lily. The realization hit him like a tidal wave, sobering him instantly. His heart raced as the pieces fell into place—Lily, his daughter. Without another word, he stood up, a man on a mission, his earlier despair replaced by a burning need to find Ava.

He navigated through the crowd, his senses heightened, until he spotted her. There she was, radiant and beautiful, standing next to her parents and Lily. At that moment, her father, James, raised his glass in a toast, his voice carrying through the room.

"Let's raise our glasses to welcome back our beloved Ava, and to introduce the newest addition to our family, my granddaughter, Lily," he announced, his voice warm with pride and affection.

The room erupted in cheers, the joyous sounds of clinking glasses and congratulations filling the space. Ethan's eyes were fixed on Ava and Lily, the sight both overwhelming and surreal. There, in the midst of celebration and family warmth, he saw his world, the one he had longed for and the one he had almost lost.

As the toast concluded and the crowd's attention shifted, Ethan took a deep breath, steadying himself for the conversation that lay ahead. With every step towards Ava and Lily, his resolve strengthened, ready to face the past, embrace the present, and hopefully, shape a future he had once thought was beyond his reach.

Ava's gaze met Ethan's across the room, and in that silent exchange, she understood—he had just discovered the truth about Lily. She watched as a myriad of emotions played across

Ethan's face. The shock, realization, and then an overwhelming joy mixed with tears. He stepped closer, his eyes never leaving Lily's face.

"Can I... Can I hold her?" Ethan's voice was barely a whisper, laden with emotion.

Ava hesitated for a moment, her heart racing. Then, with a gentle nod, she carefully handed Lily over to Ethan. "Lily, this is your daddy," she said softly.

Lily looked up at Ethan with curious eyes. "Daddy?" she echoed, her small voice filled with innocence and wonder.

Ethan, now holding his daughter for the first time, was overcome with emotion. Tears streamed down his face as he looked at Lily, then at Ava. "I... I can't believe it. She's... she's beautiful, Ava."

Ava watched them, her own tears flowing freely now. "She's been asking about you," Ava said, her voice trembling. "She wanted to know if her daddy loved her."

Ethan knelt down to be at eye level with Lily. "I love you so much, Lily," he said, his voice choked with tears. "I didn't know you existed, but I promise, I'll make up for all the lost time."

Lily, sensing the emotional gravity of the moment, wrapped her little arms around Ethan's neck. "I love you too, Daddy."

Ethan looked up at Ava, his eyes conveying a world of gratitude and love. "Thank you, Ava," he said. "Thank you for giving me the most beautiful gift. I didn't know how empty my life was until this moment."

Lily, in her innocent and trusting nature, reached out her arms towards Ethan's parents. The moment was filled with a profound tenderness as Ethan gently handed his daughter to his mother.

Ethan's mom cradled Lily, her eyes brimming with tears of happiness. "Oh, you're just as beautiful as your mommy," she cooed, gently rocking Lily in her arms. Ethan's dad stood beside them, his face aglow with a grandfather's pride, his hand tenderly stroking Lily's hair.

"Look at you, our beautiful granddaughter," he said softly, his voice thick with emotion. "We have so much to catch up on."

Lily, comfortable in her grandmother's arms, smiled and nodded, her eyes shining with curiosity and joy. "I like your necklace," she said, pointing at Ethan's mom's necklace, her childlike wonder bringing a lightness to the emotional moment.

Ethan and Ava stood there, watching the scene, their hearts filled with a mix of joy and bittersweet emotions. Ava felt a sense of relief and completion, seeing Lily being embraced by her paternal grandparents.

Ethan, standing beside Ava, reached for her hand, giving it a gentle squeeze. Their eyes met, sharing a moment of unspoken understanding and gratitude.

Ethan handed Ava a handkerchief, noticing the moisture in her eyes. "Here, you might need this," he said softly.

"Thank you," Ava replied, her voice a whisper, taking the handkerchief and dabbing her eyes.

Their moment was interrupted as Amy, Sofia, and Jasmine approached with wide smiles. "Ava! We've missed you!" Amy exclaimed, enveloping Ava in a heartfelt hug.

Jasmine added, "And Lily, she's just the cutest! We can't believe you kept her a secret."

Ava chuckled, "It's been quite a journey, you know."

Carlson, joining the group, couldn't help but ask, "So, Ava, where's your husband? Ethan mentioned something about you being married."

Ava's smile faltered slightly. "Husband? No, I'm not married. That was a misunderstanding," she clarified, glancing briefly at Ethan.

Tony nudged into the conversation with a hint of mischief. "Ethan here was pretty convinced you'd moved on."

Ethan, looking a bit embarrassed, gently nudged Tony, signaling him to change the subject.

"I guess I was wrong," Ava said, trying to maintain a light tone. "No husband, just me and Lily."

The mood shifted slightly as Carlson, perhaps teasingly, ventured, "So, any chance you and Ethan might... you know, rekindle things?"

A pause hung in the air, all eyes turning to Ava. She looked at Ethan, their gazes meeting in a moment of unspoken communication, before she turned back to her friends. "I... I don't think so," she said, her voice wavering slightly, a mix of sadness and resignation in her tone.

Ethan's expression changed subtly, a hint of pain crossing his features. Ava noticed but quickly looked away, feeling a pang of guilt.

Amy, sensing the growing awkwardness, whispered to Carlson, "Maybe that wasn't the best thing to bring up right now."

Carlson scratched his head, looking apologetic. "Yeah, my bad. Sorry, guys."

Ethan remained silent, lost in his thoughts, as Ava forced a smile, trying to shift the focus away from their complicated past. The friends, picking up on the sensitive nature of the conversation, tactfully steered the topic towards more neutral ground, but the weight of Ava's words lingered, leaving an unspoken tension in the air.

Ethan remained quiet, his thoughts swirling in the aftermath of the party. Holding Lily in his arms, he followed Ava to her room, gently laying their daughter on the bed. After tucking Lily in and kissing her forehead, a profound silence filled the room, weighing heavily between him and Ava.

Breaking the silence with a hesitant voice, Ethan asked, "Can I... visit here again to spend time with Lily? Would that be okay?"

Ava met his gaze, a soft smile touching her lips. "Of course. She'd love that," she responded warmly.

"Thanks," Ethan murmured, grateful yet somber. After a moment, he sighed heavily, his voice laden with regret. "I'm sorry, Ava."

Ava, puzzled, turned to face him. "For what?"

"For hurting you, five years ago. For everything that led to... this." His eyes, filled with remorse, locked onto hers.

Ava's breath caught in her throat. Standing, she turned away, trying to compose herself. "Ethan, that was five years ago. It's all in the past. I left because I thought you were happy with Violet."

Ethan approached her, his touch gentle on her shoulders. "But it's never just been in the past for me," he confessed, his voice trembling with emotion. "I've regretted letting you go every single day."

Ava's heart raced. "After you left that morning, I was lost. I looked for you, called, but you were gone. I've been living in a void ever since."

Turning Ava to face him, Ethan saw her tears. Gently wiping them away, he pleaded, "Please, don't close the door on us. I love you, baby. I don't want to lose you or Lily again."

"I'm afraid, Ethan," she sobbed, her voice trembling. "Afraid of getting hurt, of making the wrong choice for Lily and me."

Ethan embraced her, his own tears mingling with hers. "I know, baby, I know. But please, give me a chance to make everything right. Let me show you how much I love you, how much I've missed you."

Ava's hands clutched at his tux, her heart torn between fear and a love that never waned. In his embrace, she found a flicker of hope, a chance for a new beginning.

Ever since the revelation at the Christmas party, Ethan had been on a mission to mend the broken bridges between him and Ava. His determination was evident in every bouquet of flowers that arrived at Ava's patisserie, each one a silent plea for forgiveness, a testament to his unwavering resolve to make amends. He had also become a regular visitor to the shop, not just as a suitor trying to win Ava back, but as a father eager to make up for the lost time with Lily.

One day, Ethan entered the shop, his arms laden with flowers and a carefully chosen assortment of gifts for Ava, all handpicked with Lily's help. His heart swelled with anticipation, envisioning Ava's smile, the softening of her eyes that he longed to see again. But as he stepped inside, the scene before him was a sharp jolt back to reality.

There sat Brian, relaxed and at ease, sharing a comfortable moment with Ava. The sight of them so close, so natural together, sent a pang of jealousy through Ethan. But it was the sound of Lily's cheerful voice that truly twisted the knife. "Daddy Brian!" she called out, running towards Brian with the unrestrained joy of a child greeting a beloved figure in her life.

Ethan clenched his jaw, the effort to keep his emotions in check evident as he approached Ava and Brian. "You're here again," he remarked, directing his comment towards Brian, his tone a thinly veiled attempt to mask the swirling mix of jealousy and frustration within him. Despite this, he put on a wide smile as he extended the flowers and gifts towards Ava.

Ava glanced up, her face a calm mask, yet Ethan could sense the underlying tension. "Ethan, you didn't have to bring all these," she said, acknowledging the thoughtful gesture but maintaining a composed distance.

Brian, momentarily pulling his attention away from Lily, met Ethan's gaze squarely. There was a calmness in his demeanor, but the underlying message was clear—this was his territory too. "Ethan, good to see you again," he said, his voice even but carrying an undercurrent of rivalry. "I came to see Lily if that's alright."

Ava quickly smoothed over the brewing tension with a warm smile, her voice inclusive. "Of course it's alright, Bri. You've helped me raise Lily after all," she chimed in, her gratitude towards Brian evident.

Ethan's gaze shifted between Ava and Brian, the sight of them together igniting a fierce determination within him. "I see you and Brian have gotten quite close," he remarked, his voice tinged with a mixture of inquiry and concealed pain.

Ava's eyes met his, her response measured yet revealing. "Brian has been a great friend, especially in times when Lily and I needed support," she said, her words a subtle acknowledgment of the bond they shared.

Brian's agreement, his tone friendly yet underscored with a firmness, was a testament to the shared history between him and Ava. "We've been through a lot together. It's only natural," he said, his gaze briefly meeting Ethan's.

In that moment, Ethan realized the extent of what he had missed, the life that had unfolded in his absence. The urge to stay, to fight for his place in their lives, warred with the realization that his presence was, for now, an intrusion into the delicate balance Ava had built.

"I'll go ahead," Ethan said abruptly, his voice steady but the sadness in his eyes betraying his true feelings. The patisserie, once a symbol of potential reconciliation, now felt like a reminder of all he had lost.

Ava's simple acknowledgment, "Sure," was polite but distant, a clear signal that the path to forgiveness was still long and uncertain.

As he turned to leave, Lily's cheerful "Goodbye, Daddy!" reached his ears, a bittersweet note that resonated deep within him. He waved back, a smile on his lips but a heaviness in his heart.

CHAPTER NINETEEN

In the weeks following Ethan's realization about Lily, he had thrown himself into a relentless pursuit of reconciliation with Ava. Despite her polite but distant demeanor, he remained undeterred, understanding that the years of pain and solitude she endured because of him couldn't be healed overnight. Ava, for her part, maintained a careful distance, her interactions with Ethan marked by a cautious detachment—a barrier erected to protect her still-mending heart.

The patisserie had become a battleground of emotions, with Ethan's frequent visits a constant reminder of the delicate dance they were navigating. Each time he walked through the door, Ava felt a familiar tug in her heart, a mix of old affections and the stark reminder of past hurts. She often busied herself with customers or retreated to the kitchen, her actions a silent plea for the space she needed to sort through the whirlwind of emotions Ethan's presence evoked.

At her parents' house, the dynamics were similar. Ethan's attempts to integrate himself back into the family were met with Ava's polite but firm boundaries. She would engage in conversation only when necessary, her responses measured, her smiles careful and guarded. Ethan recognized the walls she had built around herself, a fortress to safeguard the fragile peace she had found.

It was during a camping barbecue trip that the delicate balance they had maintained was put to the test. The air was filled with the scent of roasting marshmallows and the crackling of the campfire.

As the evening chill descended upon the campsite, Ethan and Ava sat by the crackling bonfire, the glow of the flames casting a warm light on their faces. Lily had fallen asleep, her gentle breathing a quiet reminder of the new bond that had brought them all together. Ethan, his heart heavy with a mixture of hope and apprehension, draped a wool blanket over Ava's shoulders before sitting beside her.

"Thank you for agreeing to this camping trip, Ava," Ethan began, his voice soft as he carefully roasted marshmallows over the fire. "Are you having fun?"

Ava's response was straightforward, her tone neutral. "Lily wanted to come, so I really had no choice but to join as well," she said, her words unintentionally stinging Ethan.

Ethan sighed, the weight of their past and his longing to make things right pressing down on him. "Ava, I know you have every reason to keep your distance," he said earnestly, the firelight reflecting the sincerity in his eyes. "I understand the pain I've caused, and I don't expect instant forgiveness. But every moment away from you, every moment I missed with Lily, it weighs on me. I'm here to make things right, to be the father Lily deserves and the man you once believed in."

Ava remained silent, her gaze locked on the dancing flames, the light casting shadows on her conflicted face. Ethan, undeterred, continued to pour his heart out. "This camping trip, being with you and Lily, it's a stark reminder of everything I've missed. I'm not asking to reclaim my place in your heart overnight, Ava. All I'm asking for is a chance to show you, day by day, that I'm worthy of being part of your life again."

Ava's voice was quiet but firm when she finally spoke. "I came to tell you that I've decided to go back to Ketchikan with Lily. We've built a life there, and we're happy," she revealed, her words cutting through the night air.

Ethan's heart shattered at her words, his eyes a mirror of the pain and desperation he felt. "You really want to get away from me that bad, huh?" he asked, his voice a raw whisper.

In the flickering light, Ava saw the tears welling up in Ethan's eyes, the heartbreak evident in his gaze. "Please, Ava, tell me what I need to do to make you stay. I'll do anything," Ethan pleaded, his voice breaking.

Without a word, Ava watched as Ethan moved closer, sitting on the ground before her, his face a canvas of fear and longing.

"I just got you back... I don't want to lose you again," he choked out, his emotions spilling over. "Please forgive me. I swear I won't ever break your heart again."

Ethan's tears flowed freely, his hand reaching out to touch her face gently. "I'd move to Ketchikan if that's what it takes. I'll go wherever you both are. Just... tell me you want me in your life again. I love you so much, Ava."

In that moment, under the starlit sky, with the fire crackling and Ethan's heartfelt pleas hanging in the air, Ava felt her resolve waver. Yet, despite the tumult of emotions within her, she knew she couldn't simply erase the past. Her decision to return to Ketchikan was not just about distance—it was about protecting the fragile peace she had fought so hard to build for herself and Lily.

Ethan's groveling, his raw display of vulnerability and love, tugged at her heartstrings, but Ava remained silent, her mind made up, even as her heart ached at the sight of his pain. The road to healing and forgiveness was long, and while Ethan's words offered a glimmer of hope, Ava knew that some wounds required more than promises—they needed time, space, and, above all, a trust that had to be rebuilt from the ground up.

Few days following the camping trip, a thick silence enveloped Ava's world. Ethan, once a persistent presence in her life, had vanished without a trace. Messages went unanswered, calls unreturned. Even Nate, usually so attuned to his friend's movements, expressed concern. Ethan's sudden and uncharacteristic leave of absence from work only deepened the worry.

Ava, despite her resolve to maintain distance, found herself increasingly anxious. The thought that her decision to leave might have driven Ethan into this reclusive state weighed heavily on her. The more she considered it, the more the need to ensure his well-being gnawed at her.

Finally, she reached out to Nate, her voice tense with concern. "Nate, where does Ethan live? It's been almost a week, and no one's heard from him. I need to check on him."

Nate hesitated, the gravity of the situation evident in his voice. "He's still in the apartment in Manhattan. He never moved, Ava. After you left, he... he couldn't bring himself to leave. Said it was the last place he felt connected to you."

Ava's heart clenched at the revelation, a mix of guilt and a newfound urgency propelling her forward. "I need to see him, Nate. I can't just sit here not knowing if he's okay."

Nate's next words were spoken softly, a truth only he knew, one that Ethan had kept hidden in the depths of his heart. "Ava, there's something you should know. After you left, Ethan... he was a shell of the man he used to be. He threw himself into work, avoided social gatherings, anything that might remind him too much of you. But no matter how hard he tried, he couldn't escape the memories. Your picture, the one from your anniversary, it's still on his nightstand. He kept hoping, waiting for a sign that you might come back."

The image of a solitary Ethan, living in the shadow of their shared past, struck a chord within Ava. The man who had once broken her heart now seemed to be breaking his own, holding onto the fragments of a life they once dreamed of together.

"He's serious about winning you back, Ava. He's changed a lot," Nate added, his voice earnest. "He's been patient, respectful of your space, but his feelings... they've never wavered. He still loves you, deeply."

Nate's voice softened, a brother's insight into his sister's heart coming to the forefront. "And Ava, I know you still love him. I see it in the way you speak about him, in the way you worry. There's nothing standing in your way now. No misunderstandings, no secrets. Just two people who've been given a second chance to make things right."

With Nate's words echoing in her mind, Ava knew she couldn't delay any longer. The need to see Ethan, to confront the past and face whatever remained of their connection, was no longer a choice—it was a necessity.

Ava, her heart racing with a mix of anticipation and apprehension, sped through the streets of New York towards their old apartment. Her tears flowed freely, blurring the city lights as she drove. The voicemails Ethan had left over the years filled the car, each word tugging at her heartstrings.

'Hey baby, it's me again. I don't even know if you're listening to these since it's been two years since you left me, but I have to talk to you, even if it's just into this phone. I walked through Central Park today, and I swear, every corner, every bench had a memory of us. I keep seeing you everywhere, in every smile, every laugh that echoes ours. It's hard, baby... it's hard without you. I miss you more than words can say. I keep wondering if you ever think of me, if New York reminds you of me like it does of you for me. Anyway, I just wanted to share that. I hope you're well, wherever you are.'

'Baby, it's Ethan again. Four years... it's been four years, and I still find myself reaching for my phone to tell you about my day. I wonder how you are, if you've moved on. Are you happy? That's all I ever wanted for you. If you've found someone else, if you're smiling and in love, then I'm happy for you, truly. Just know that you'll always have a special place in my heart. You were my everything, Ava. I guess a part of me will always be waiting for you.'

Tears streamed down Ava's face as she drove, her hands trembling slightly on the steering wheel. The raw emotion in Ethan's voice, the evident longing and love, resonated with every fiber of her being. She needed to see him, to talk to him, to explain everything. Her heart raced with anticipation and a deep, unresolved love as she neared their old apartment.

As Ava stood in the doorway of their old apartment, her heart heavy with emotion, Ethan dropped the trash bags and approached her with a look of deep concern. "Ava, what's wrong? Why are you crying?" His voice was filled with worry.

Ava, tears streaming down her face, stepped inside, her back to Ethan. The weight of the past and the uncertainty of the future mingled in her heart. "You've hurt me so much, Ethan... I became too scared to even think about loving you again," she sobbed, her voice trembling.

Ethan's expression was pained as he stepped closer. "Babe, I'm—"

Ava turned to face him, her tears unabated. "But the truth is... I never stopped loving you, Ethan. My love for you only grew stronger after having Lily. She reminds me of you every day."

Ava's voice trembled as she spoke, her emotions raw and exposed. "I wanted so badly to be mad at you, for the hurt you caused me. But no matter how hard I tried, I couldn't bring myself to stay angry. From the very first day I saw you in college, I've been hopelessly in love with you. I used to daydream about being your wife, having a family with you, even when you were looking elsewhere."

She bit her lip, a wave of nostalgia washing over her. "And when you finally asked me out, it felt like a dream come true. I made a vow to myself to be the best for you, to love you wholeheartedly, so you'd never have any regrets about choosing me."

Tears streamed down her cheeks as painful memories surfaced. "I gave you everything, Ethan, and in return, you broke my heart. The pain you and Violet caused me... it was unbearable. But even after all that, I find myself here, unable to let go, still deeply in love with you." Ava's voice cracked with the weight of her unshed tears, her heart laid bare in front of Ethan.

"Sometimes I think I'm so stupid because---"

Before Ava could finish her sentence, Ethan closed the gap between them, his actions driven by a yearning that had been building for years. He kissed her deeply, pouring every ounce of his pent-up emotions into the embrace.

He cradled her face in his hands with such gentleness, as if she were the most precious thing in the world. Their eyes met in a moment of profound understanding, speaking volumes of unspoken love and longing.

"I love you, Ava," Ethan whispered, his voice laden with emotion. He kissed her again, this time pouring all his pent-up feelings into it. The kiss deepened, becoming more passionate as Ava responded, her own emotions surfacing.

The room was filled with the unspoken words of their hearts, their kiss bridging the years of separation and hurt. In that moment, all the pain and uncertainty seemed to dissolve, leaving only the pure, undeniable love they had for each other.

As they lay together, wrapped in each other's embrace, Ethan's request was simple yet filled with longing. "Stay with me tonight..." His eyes conveyed a depth of affection and a plea for her presence.

Ava, still caught in the afterglow of their passionate reunion, chuckled softly, a mix of joy and practicality in her voice. "Lily might wake up and look for me. I have to go home tonight."

Ethan, not willing to let the moment end, playfully countered, "But you are home, babe. This is our apartment." He gazed at her with a look that was half playful, half earnest, his lips pressing a gentle kiss on her shoulder.

Their eyes met, a silent conversation unfolding between them. Ava felt a surge of emotions, her heart agreeing before her mind. "Okay," she whispered, her smile mirroring Ethan's joy.

His reaction was instant, a mixture of surprise and elation. "Really?" Ethan's voice was filled with excitement as he sat up, leaning over her. "No changing your mind, okay?"

"I won't. I swear," Ava replied, her laughter mingling with his, a sound that filled the room with warmth.

Ethan's grin turned mischievous as he leaned in closer, his breath tickling her neck. "But for tonight, you're all mine. Let's make the most of it while our daughter isn't here." He began to shower her with playful kisses, eliciting peals of laughter from Ava.

The apartment was alive with their laughter and joy, a testament to their rekindled love. And as the night deepened, they once again found themselves lost in each other, their love reaffirmed with every touch, every kiss, every shared moment, undisturbed by the world outside.

Ava awoke the next morning feeling a delightful mix of happiness and soreness, a testament to the passion they had rekindled the night before. "Good morning, sunshine," Ethan greeted her with a soft voice, lying comfortably beside her.

She blushed, feeling slightly shy and covered herself with the blanket. Ethan's chuckle filled the room as he gently pulled the blanket away from her face. "I love seeing you blush, babe. You're so pretty," he said, his eyes shining with sincerity.

"When did you wake up?" Ava asked, her voice still carrying a hint of sleep.

"A couple of hours ago," Ethan replied with a grin. "I made breakfast for us. But first, I want to show you something special," he added, his eyes gleaming with excitement.

Curious, Ava quickly got dressed and followed Ethan to the next room. As the door opened, she was greeted by a breathtaking sight. The guest room had been transformed into a little girl's paradise. Stuffed toys were arranged in a playful ensemble, and a charming dollhouse stood proudly in one corner. The bed was adorned with a beautiful set, perfect for a young girl, and the wallpaper was a gentle pink adorned with delicate images of pink lilies.

Ava's eyes widened in amazement. "Ethan, this is incredible! When did you manage to do all of this?" she exclaimed, her voice filled with admiration and surprise.

"I've been completely wrapped up in fixing up the house for the past few days, especially getting Lily's room ready," Ethan explained, his voice tinged with excitement. "And it's not just her room – I've overhauled the kitchen and living room too. I wanted to ensure everything was childproof and welcoming." Ethan said, a proud smile on his face.

"I wanted to prepare a special place for Lily, just in case you decided to come home. It was meant to be a surprise for both of you," he chuckled, his eyes twinkling playfully.

He gave a sheepish grin, pulling out his phone. "In all the chaos of renovation, I completely lost track of my phone. Look, it's even dead," he chuckled, showing her the unresponsive screen. "I'm really sorry for not staying in touch these last few days, babe. It wasn't intentional, I promise you that."

Ava embraced him, overwhelmed with gratitude and love. "Thank you, Ethan. Lily will absolutely love this," she said, kissing him gently on the cheek.

As Ethan gazed at her, his eyes reflected a deep love and a promise of a future together. Ava's heart swelled with joy.

"We should head to my parents' house soon," Ava said, suddenly remembering Lily. "She might be wondering where I am." Quickly, they made their way to the kitchen, where Ethan had prepared a lovely breakfast. As they ate, Ava felt an overwhelming sense of contentment, knowing they were finally a family again.

Ethan and Ava drove back to her parents' house, Ava feeling a mix of excitement and nervousness about telling her family their decision. As they arrived at the mansion, Ethan reassuringly held her hand as they entered. Inside, they heard the delightful sound of Lily's laughter coming from the living room.

Upon seeing her parents, Lily ran over, her arms wide open. "Mommy! Mommy, you're back!" she squealed with joy, her bright eyes shining. "And Daddy's here too!"

Ethan bent down, scooping Lily into his arms with a wide smile. "Hey, peanut. How are you?" he asked tenderly.

"I'm okay, Daddy. But I missed you so bad! You didn't come visit Lily yesterday," Lily pouted, her little face showing a hint of sadness.

"I missed you too, peanut," he said warmly.

Nate's teasing voice broke the tender moment. "So, how did it go last night?" he asked with a wink. "Ava, you didn't come home. You and Ethan are back together, aren't you?"

Ava blushed, meeting her brother's gaze shyly. Their parents looked on with a mix of amusement and anticipation.

"Ethan, Ava," Ava's father began, his voice firm yet filled with warmth. "What's going on? Is there something you'd like to share?"

"Let's go and have some fun in the garden, Lily flower," Nate suggested, scooping up his niece with a gentle smile. He sensed the importance of the moment unfolding between Ava and Ethan and decided to give them some space. With Lily in his arms, he headed towards the garden, leaving Ava, Ethan, and their parents in the living room for a private conversation.

Ethan, holding Ava's hand, gently guided her to sit across her parents. He took a deep breath, his expression serious.

Ethan cleared his throat, meeting the gaze of Ava's parents with a solemn look. "Mr. and Mrs. Greenwood, I'm here today to speak about something that's deeply important to me and

Ava. We've been through a lot, and after everything, we've realized that we still love each other. Last night, Ava and I made the decision to give our relationship another chance."

He paused, a hint of vulnerability in his eyes. "But I'm not here just to say this. I need to acknowledge the hurt I've caused Ava, and by extension, you both. I wasn't there for her when she needed me most, and I know that's something I can never take back. I understand I might have lost your trust because of my actions."

His voice was steady but filled with emotion. "I'm not asking for immediate forgiveness, but rather a chance to earn back your trust. I want to be the man Ava deserves and the father Lily needs. I'm here to ask for your blessing to love Ava again and to be part of this family. I promise, with all that I am, to cherish, support, and stand by Ava and Lily. They mean everything to me." Ethan's words conveyed his deep remorse and commitment to making amends.

Ava's father listened intently, his expression softening as he took in Ethan's words. After a moment of thoughtful silence, he spoke, his voice calm yet carrying a weight of sincerity. "Ethan, we never held any anger towards you. Ava made us promise not to. She knew that if we harbored any resentment, it would only hurt her more."

He leaned forward slightly, his gaze steady on Ethan. "I won't deny that I was disappointed. I entrusted you with the most precious person in my life, my daughter, and you let her down. That was hard for us to see."

The room was quiet, the air heavy with unspoken emotions. "But," he continued, "in these past years, I've seen the pain and regret in your eyes. I've seen how lost you were without Ava and how much you still cared for her, even after all this time. That's not something a father can ignore."

His voice softened further, a mix of understanding and fatherly concern. "You've made your mistakes, Ethan, but I believe in giving people a chance to make things right. If my daughter believes in you, then I'm willing to put my trust in you again. Just remember, Ava and Lily are the most important people in this room, and they deserve all the love and care you can give." His words carried a father's protective love, but also an openness to forgiveness and moving forward.

Ava's mother's question lingered in the air, her eyes reflecting a mix of hope and concern. "So, what's next for you two? Are you starting over, or...?" she trailed off, leaving the question open-ended.

Ethan, feeling the weight of the moment, turned to Ava and then addressed her parents with a clear and unwavering voice. "Ava and I have had enough time apart to know exactly what we want. I don't want to waste another day without her as my wife. If it were up to me, I'd marry her tomorrow."

A soft chuckle filled the room, lightening the moment. Ava's mother smiled, a twinkle in her eyes. Ava, feeling a surge of love and gratitude towards Ethan, spoke up, "We've decided to talk things through more thoroughly and also to discuss with Ethan's parents. But yes, we are planning to get married soon. We'll set the date once everything's sorted out."

Her father nodded thoughtfully, his expression one of contentment. "That's good to hear. What matters most is that you both are sure about this decision."

The conversation flowed more freely after that, the room filled with a sense of warmth and family.

The day following her reconciliation with Ethan, Ava felt a compelling urge to speak with Brian. She believed that of all people, he deserved to hear her decision firsthand, considering the profound role he had played in her and Lily's life. With a sense of purpose and a heart heavy with mixed emotions, Ava reached out and asked Brian to meet her at her shop.

Ava sat across from Brian in the quiet of her shop, the familiar surroundings a stark contrast to the tumultuous emotions swirling within her. She took a deep breath, searching for the words to convey what her heart had decided, but before she could speak, Brian's gentle chuckle broke the silence.

"You and Ethan have gotten back together, right?" he asked, his voice tinged with a sweetness that carried an undercurrent of sorrow.

The dam within Ava broke at his words, tears cascading down her cheeks as the reality of the situation crashed over her. "I... I'm sorry, Brian... I never meant to hurt you," she stammered between sobs, the weight of her decision pressing heavily upon her.

Brian's response was a testament to his character, his voice soft and reassuring as he took her hand in his. "Hey, it's okay," he said, locking eyes with her, his gaze void of resentment, filled instead with empathy. "You don't have to feel bad, Ava. I knew where I stood in your life when I chose to share my feelings. And you, you gave me a chance. You opened up, even when it was hard. That means everything to me."

Ava's tears flowed freely, each drop a mix of relief and guilt. How could someone as kind and understanding as Brian endure such pain with such grace?

Brian offered her a warm, comforting smile, his thumb gently wiping away her tears. "Don't cry, Ava. Being true to yourself, to your heart, that's what matters most. And I'll be okay, I promise," he assured her, his voice a steady presence in the storm of her emotions.

The conversation that followed was a bittersweet symphony of gratitude, understanding, and the recognition of an unbreakable bond forged through years of friendship and mutual support. As they talked, they acknowledged the unique place they held in each other's lives, a place that, while forever altered, would always be cherished.

As they prepared to part ways, a mutual understanding passed between them. "Brian, you'll always be a part of Lily's life. She adores you... 'Daddy Brian,'" Ava said, a small smile breaking through her tears.

Brian nodded, his own smile bittersweet but genuine. "And I wouldn't have it any other way. Lily is a special girl, and I care about her deeply. Just like I care about you, Ava. Always remember that."

They stood, their goodbye a poignant moment filled with promises of continued friendship and unwavering support. As Brian walked away, Ava knew that while the chapters of their lives were turning, the story they shared, the bond they had, would endure—transformed, perhaps, but never diminished. And in that knowledge, there was a comfort, a quiet strength that would carry them both forward into the unknown paths of the future.

CHAPTER TWENTY

The garden of the Greenwood residence was transformed into a picturesque wedding venue, with the intimate gathering of their closest friends and family adding to the warmth and love that filled the air. The sun was setting, casting a golden hue over the event, making it even more magical.

Ava stood at the entrance, looking radiant in her wedding dress. The gown was simple yet strikingly elegant, hugging her figure gracefully. It was a classic A-line silhouette with delicate lace detailing and a modest train that flowed behind her. Her hair was styled in a chic updo, with a few loose strands framing her face. A light veil completed her look, adding an ethereal quality to her presence.

Ethan waited at the altar, looking dapper in his tailored suit. The dark hue of his suit contrasted perfectly with the soft colors of the garden, making him stand out. His eyes were fixed on Ava, a mixture of awe and love evident in his gaze.

As the ceremony began, their daughter Lily, dressed in a cute white dress with a sash matching Ava's gown, made her way down the aisle as the flower girl. She scattered petals with a big smile on her face, her excitement palpable.

When Ava reached Ethan, they exchanged vows that they had written for each other. Ava took a deep breath before speaking, her voice filled with emotion.

"Ethan, in front of our family, friends, and most importantly, in front of our daughter Lily, I promise to love and cherish you every day. I vow to support you, to challenge you, and to grow with you. You are my heart, my soul, my everything. You've shown me that true love withstands any obstacle, and for that, I am forever grateful. I promise to be there for you, in laughter and in tears, in sickness and in health. I love you, now and always."

Ethan, visibly moved by her words, took her hands in his. "Ava, today I make a promise to you, a promise that I will spend the rest of my days keeping. I promise to be the husband you deserve, to be there for you and our beautiful daughter, Lily. I vow to cherish every moment we have together, to be your strength when you need it, and to always make our family my priority. You've given me the greatest gift by coming back into my life, and I promise to make you feel loved and cherished every single day. You are my love, my light, and my forever."

As they exchanged rings, there was hardly a dry eye among the guests. The love between Ava and Ethan was palpable, a testament to the enduring power of love and second chances. The ceremony concluded with a joyous kiss, marking the beginning of their new journey together as a family. The celebration that followed was filled with laughter, tears of happiness, and an overwhelming sense of love and unity.

The morning after their intimate and heartfelt wedding, Ethan and Ava found themselves at the airport, ready to embark on their honeymoon to the Maldives. The air was filled with a bittersweet mixture of excitement and a slight tinge of sadness as they prepared to leave their daughter Lily behind for a week.

Standing outside the departure gate, they shared a warm, loving moment with their parents and Lily. The little girl was in high spirits, seemingly understanding the special nature of this trip for her parents.

"Mommy, Daddy, promise to call me every day?" Lily asked, her big eyes looking up at them earnestly.

"Of course, peanut," Ethan replied, kneeling down to her level. "We'll tell you all about the beautiful beaches and the fish we see in the ocean."

Ava knelt beside them, gently brushing Lily's hair. "And we'll bring you back the prettiest shells we can find," she added with a warm smile. "Remember to behave for grandma and grandpa, okay?" Ava added.

"I will, Mommy!" Lily chirped, her eyes bright. "But you have to promise to bring me a brother or sister when you come back!" Her innocent request, so earnestly made, brought a burst of laughter from everyone around.

Ethan scooped Lily into his arms, giving her a big hug. "We'll see what we can do, peanut," he said with a wink, causing Lily to giggle with delight.

Ava's parents reassured the couple, "Don't worry about Lily. We'll take good care of her. You two go and enjoy your time together. You both deserve this break."

As they hugged their parents goodbye, Ava's mother whispered in her ear, "Enjoy every moment, honey. This is your time."

Ethan and Ava then made their way through the departure gate, hand in hand, both stealing glances back at their daughter and parents, their hearts full. As they walked, Ava leaned into Ethan, "I can't believe we're finally doing this."

Ethan squeezed her hand, a smile playing on his lips, "It's just the beginning of our new journey together."

Boarding the plane, they settled into their seats, both lost in thoughts of the beautiful white beaches and crystal clear waters that awaited them. The promise of a week of uninterrupted bliss in the Maldives was the perfect way to celebrate their love, a love that had endured and blossomed against all odds.

As Ava and Ethan's plane descended, the view of the Maldives from above was breathtaking. The islands dotted the Indian Ocean like emerald jewels amidst the dazzling blue waters. They landed smoothly, and a warm, tropical breeze greeted them as they exited the plane.

A short boat ride later, they arrived at their beach resort, a paradise nestled against a backdrop of clear turquoise waters and pristine white sands. The resort was a picturesque collection of nipa hut cottages on stilts, connected by wooden walkways hovering above the crystal-clear ocean.

"Our villa looks amazing!" Ava exclaimed as they approached their private nipa hut cottage. The thatched roof and the rustic exterior blended perfectly with the tranquil surroundings.

"I can't wait to explore this place," Ethan said, his eyes reflecting the shimmering ocean. "It's like something out of a dream."

As they entered their villa, the interior was a harmonious blend of traditional Maldivian style and modern luxury. The airy space was filled with natural light, and the large glass doors opened to a private deck with a breathtaking ocean view.

"Look at this view," Ava gasped, stepping onto the deck. The ocean spread out before them, a vast expanse of sparkling blue. "It's like we're floating on the ocean."

Ethan wrapped his arms around her, both of them gazing out at the horizon where the sky met the sea. "This is perfect," he whispered. "Just you, me, and the endless ocean."

Ava leaned back into him, feeling a sense of peace and contentment wash over her. "I can't believe we're here. It's so beautiful."

They spent a few moments in silence, simply absorbing the serene beauty of their surroundings. The sound of the gentle waves, the warmth of the sun, and the cool ocean breeze created an atmosphere of pure bliss.

"Let's make the most of every moment here," Ethan said, turning to face Ava with a smile. "Our honeymoon is going to be unforgettable."

Ava smiled back, her heart full. "I'm ready for every adventure with you, Ethan. This is just the beginning."

Together, hand in hand, they stepped back inside to begin their honeymoon in paradise, a world away from everything, yet closer than ever to each other.

As the evening unfolded, Ethan had a special surprise planned for Ava. He led her to an under-the-sea restaurant, a magical

THE ILLUSION OF US

place where they could dine surrounded by the wonders of the ocean. The restaurant was a large, transparent dome nestled under the sea, offering an immersive dining experience amidst the marine life.

"Wow, Ethan, this is incredible!" Ava exclaimed as they were seated at a table elegantly set with candles, creating a soft, warm glow in the underwater world. Above and around them, the ocean was alive with a mesmerizing display of aquatic animals. Schools of colorful fish swam gracefully, their vibrant colors a stark contrast against the deep blue of the sea.

A gentle, serene ambiance enveloped them as they began their meal. Each course was a culinary delight, but the real magic was in the ever-changing seascape around them. A turtle glided majestically past, its slow, deliberate movements captivating. Jellyfish pulsed rhythmically, their translucent bodies glowing faintly in the dim light.

"This is like a dream," Ava said, her eyes wide with wonder as she watched a group of fish dart playfully overhead. "I've never experienced anything like this."

Ethan reached across the table, taking her hand. "I wanted our first dinner as a married couple to be special, memorable. I'm glad you like it."

As Ava and Ethan continued to enjoy their enchanting dinner under the sea, Ava gazed up at the aquatic ballet above them, her expression turning thoughtful. "You know, I wish Lily was here with us right now. She would have been so thrilled to see all these fishes."

Ethan smiled, understanding the sentiment. "I was thinking the same. She'd be pressing her little nose against the glass, trying to count every fish," he chuckled, imagining their daughter's excitement.

"We should definitely come back here, but next time with Lily. It would be a wonderful adventure for her," Ethan suggested warmly. "Seeing her face light up at all this beauty would be priceless."

Ava's eyes lit up at the idea. "That sounds perfect. She would love that. And it would be so special, experiencing this magical place as a family."

The evening passed in a blissful blend of conversation, laughter, and exquisite food, with the ocean's beauty surrounding them. It was a perfect start to their honeymoon, a celebration of their love amidst the wonders of the Maldives.

Ethan invited Ava to join him for a late night swim in the mini pool attached to their private cottage. Changing into her black lace criss-cross bikini, Ava stepped out to the pool, immediately capturing Ethan's undivided attention.

His eyes, filled with desire, followed her every movement as she gracefully waded through the water to the other end of the pool. Ava smiled coyly at Ethan from across the pool, her silhouette illuminated by the soft moonlight. She took another sip of her wine, feeling the warmth spread through her.

Ethan, unable to resist the allure, swam towards her gracefully. "I just can't help but say it again. You are breathtaking," he said, reaching her and gently taking the wine glass from her hand, placing it safely aside.

"Flattery will get you everywhere, Mr. Williams," Ava teased, her eyes sparkling with affection and playfulness.

"You know, every time I say it, I mean it even more," Ethan said, moving closer to her through the water.

Ava took another sip of her wine, her smile teasing. "And every time you say it, I believe you a little bit more," she replied with a glint in her eye.

"You make this place even more magical, you know that?" His voice was soft but filled with emotion.

Ava placed her wine glass on the pool's edge and turned fully towards him. "And you make every moment feel like a dream," she responded.

Ethan wrapped his arms around her, pulling her close in the water. "In that case, I must be the luckiest man in the world, because being with you is exactly where I want to be," he murmured, their faces just inches apart.

Under the serene moonlit sky, Ethan leaned in closer, his lips meeting hers in a tender, brief kiss. "I love you, baby," he whispered, his eyes holding hers with an intensity that spoke volumes.

Ava's heart swelled with emotion, her voice laced with tears of joy, "Oh, Ethan, I love you too, with all of my heart." She kissed him back passionately, their connection deepening with each moment.

As Ethan's kisses grew more fervent, Ava felt a sharp gasp escape her lips when his hand gently cupped her breast, a touch filled with love and desire. Surrounded by the quiet beauty of the night, under the watchful eyes of the stars, she willingly surrendered herself to her husband, their love painting a perfect picture of passion and tenderness.

Ethan and Ava's honeymoon in the Maldives was a tapestry of romantic adventures and blissful moments. Each day brought a new experience, a new memory to cherish.

One day, they embarked on a tour to see the local sights, exploring vibrant markets and historical landmarks. Ava's eyes sparkled with curiosity as they wandered through streets filled with colorful crafts and the rich aroma of local cuisine. Ethan loved capturing her expressions, her laughter as they shared exotic fruits and delicacies.

Their scuba diving adventure was a highlight. Diving into the crystal-clear waters, they were greeted by a mesmerizing underwater world. Schools of brightly colored fish swam around them, and they marveled at the stunning coral reefs. Holding hands as they explored the depths, they felt a profound connection not just to each other, but to the natural beauty surrounding them.

As the sun set, they'd return to their cottage villa, nestled over the serene ocean. Some nights were spent on the deck, wrapped in each other's arms, watching the stars shimmer above and the gentle waves below. Other nights, they'd indulge in the luxury of their villa, making love and talking until the early hours of the morning. Each night ended with the promise of another day of love and exploration.

Their time in the Maldives was more than just a honeymoon; it was a reaffirmation of their love and a celebration of their new life together. As they packed to leave, they promised each other to come back, next time with Lily, to share the magic of this place with her. Their hearts were full, not just of love for each other, but of excitement for the future they were building together.

Ethan and Ava had just tucked Lily into bed, kissing their daughter goodnight as she drifted off to sleep. The moment they stepped out of Lily's room, Ava was struck by a sudden wave of nausea. She clutched her mouth, her face visibly pale.

"Babe, are you okay?" Ethan's voice was laced with worry as he noticed her discomfort.

Ava gave a weak nod, trying to steady herself. Ethan, ever the caring husband, gently guided her to their bedroom, helping her sit down on the bed while holding her hand reassuringly.

The thought dawned on him, a mixture of hope and excitement in his voice. "Could it be... are you pregnant?"

Ava's eyes widened, realization dawning on her as well. She'd been feeling unwell for a few days now, but she hadn't connected the dots until this moment. Without a word, she made her way to the bathroom and retrieved a pregnancy test kit from the cabinet. Ethan waited outside, his heart racing with a blend of nerves and anticipation.

Finally, Ava emerged, holding the pregnancy test in her trembling hands. The tears in her eyes spoke volumes as she showed Ethan the result - the word 'Pregnant' clearly displayed.

Ethan's reaction was immediate and joyous. He scooped Ava up in his arms, spinning her around as a laugh of pure happiness escaped him. "I can't believe it, I'm going to be a dad again!" His voice was filled with elation as he gently set her back on her feet.

Their happiness filled the room, tangible and heartwarming. Ethan wrapped his arms around her again, kissing her forehead tenderly. "I love you, babe."

"I love you too," Ava replied, her voice soft and content. She rested her head against his chest, feeling the steady beat of his heart. They were already planning to visit an OB-GYN the next morning to confirm her pregnancy, and the anticipation made the prospect of morning all the more exciting.

In that serene moment, with the quiet of the night around them and the prospect of a new life ahead, Ethan and Ava stood together, united in their love and the joy of their growing family.

###END###.

If you enjoyed this story, you might be intrigued to explore a different path in the alternate version, which takes our characters in new and unexpected directions. Dive into the alternate storyline to discover more layers and possibilities!

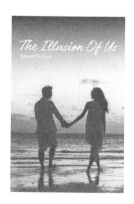

Made in the USA
Middletown, DE
08 September 2024

59961690R00146